Boys for a **The** Better World

GOOD GUYS AGENCY

Kind Like Fred Rogers

To Carter, Maxwell, Quinn, and Cora.
Whoever you choose to be, be kind.
—N. E.

BUSHEL
& PECK
BOOKS

Text copyright © 2022 by Nick Esposito
Illustration copyright © 2022 by Ricardo Tokumoto

Published by Bushel & Peck Books, a family-run publishing house in Fresno, California, that
believes in uplifting children with the highest standards of art, music, literature, and ideas.
Find beautiful books for gifted young minds at www.bushelandpeckbooks.com.

Type set in LTC Kennerly Pro, Pilkius Romeus, and Impact Label
Some visual elements licensed from Shutterstock.com
Sources consulted: *Kindness and Wonder: Why Mister Rogers Matters
Now More Than Ever* by Gavin Edwards

Bushel & Peck Books is dedicated to fighting illiteracy all over the world. For every book we
sell, we donate one to a child in need—book for book. To nominate a school or organization to
receive free books, please visit www.bushelandpeckbooks.com.

LCCN: 2022936074
ISBN: 9781638190790

First Edition

Printed in China

10 9 8 7 6 5 4 3 2 1

Better World

GOOD GUYS AGENCY

Kind like Fred Rogers

Nick Esposito • Illustrated by Ricardo Tokumoto

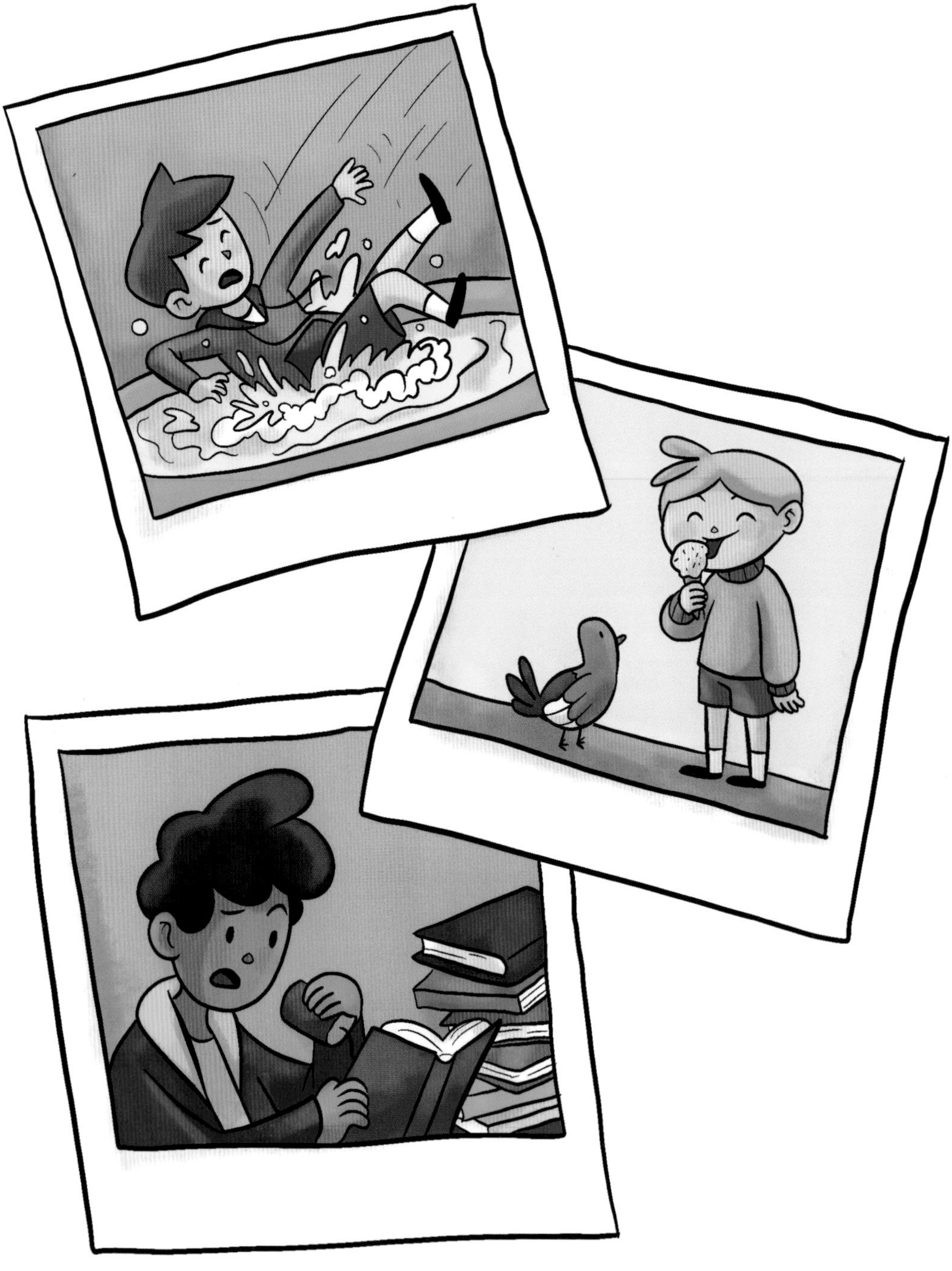

Contents

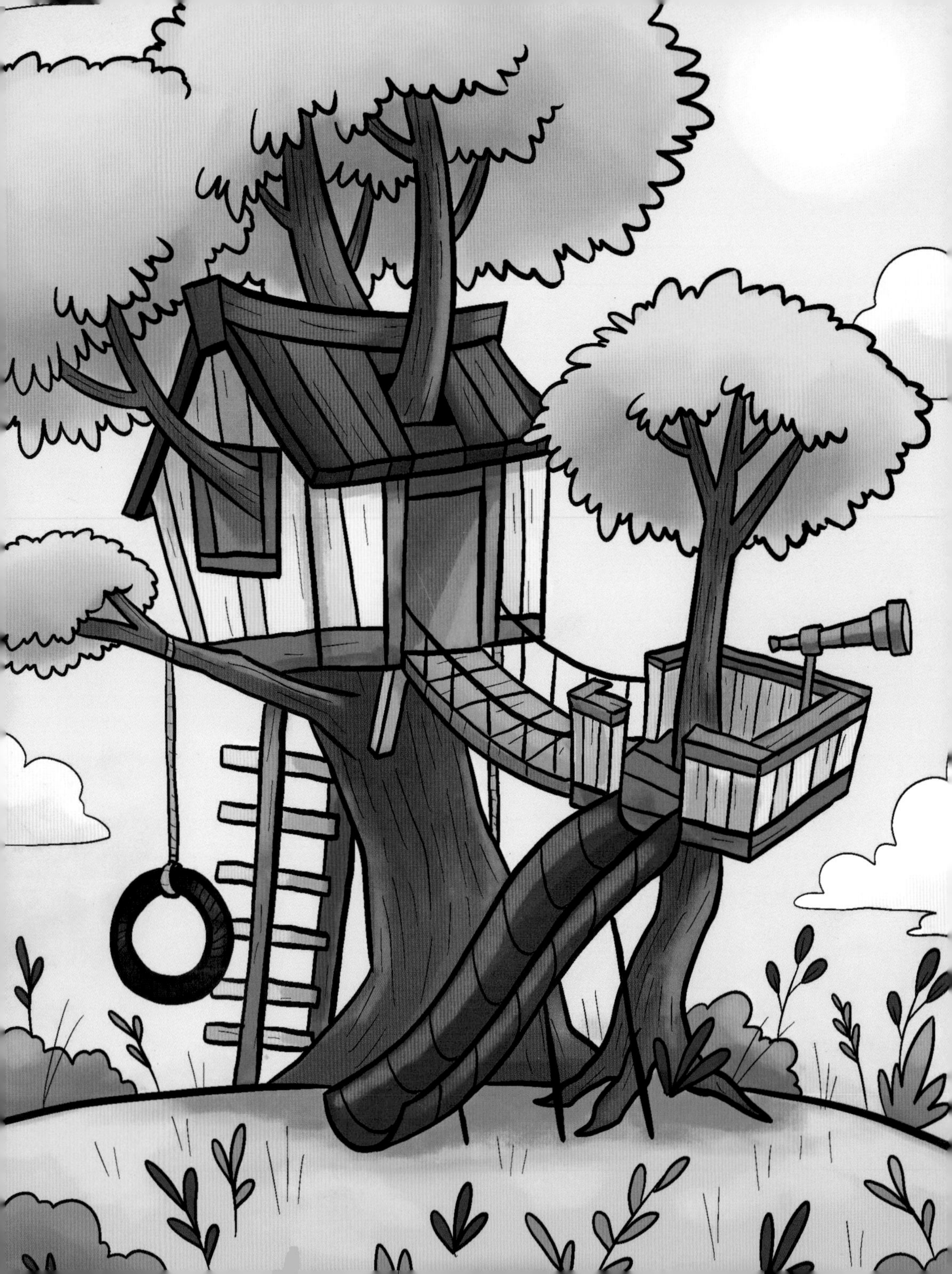

CHAPTER ONE

The Good Guys Agency

It was a Saturday morning, and Lucky was on his soapbox . . . again.

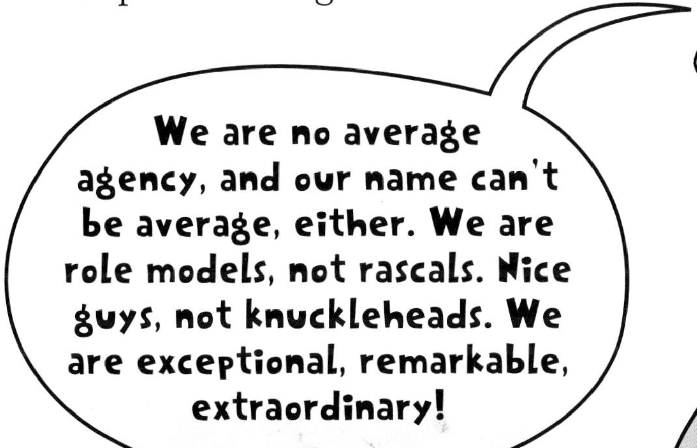

> We are no average agency, and our name can't be average, either. We are role models, not rascals. Nice guys, not knuckleheads. We are exceptional, remarkable, extraordinary!

Rudy yawned. "I'm pretty sure all those words mean the same thing. What about just *good*?"

"Rudy, I've just had the most *brilliant* idea," Lucky said. "GOOD! Now that's a word for who we are. The *Good Guys*."

Superb. That only took us an hour to come up with.

"YES!" Lucky said, paying no notice. "The Good Guys *Agency*. Isn't that perfect?"

"But can we have a proper agency with just two people?"

There was an unusual silence as Lucky paused to consider. But then, from down below:

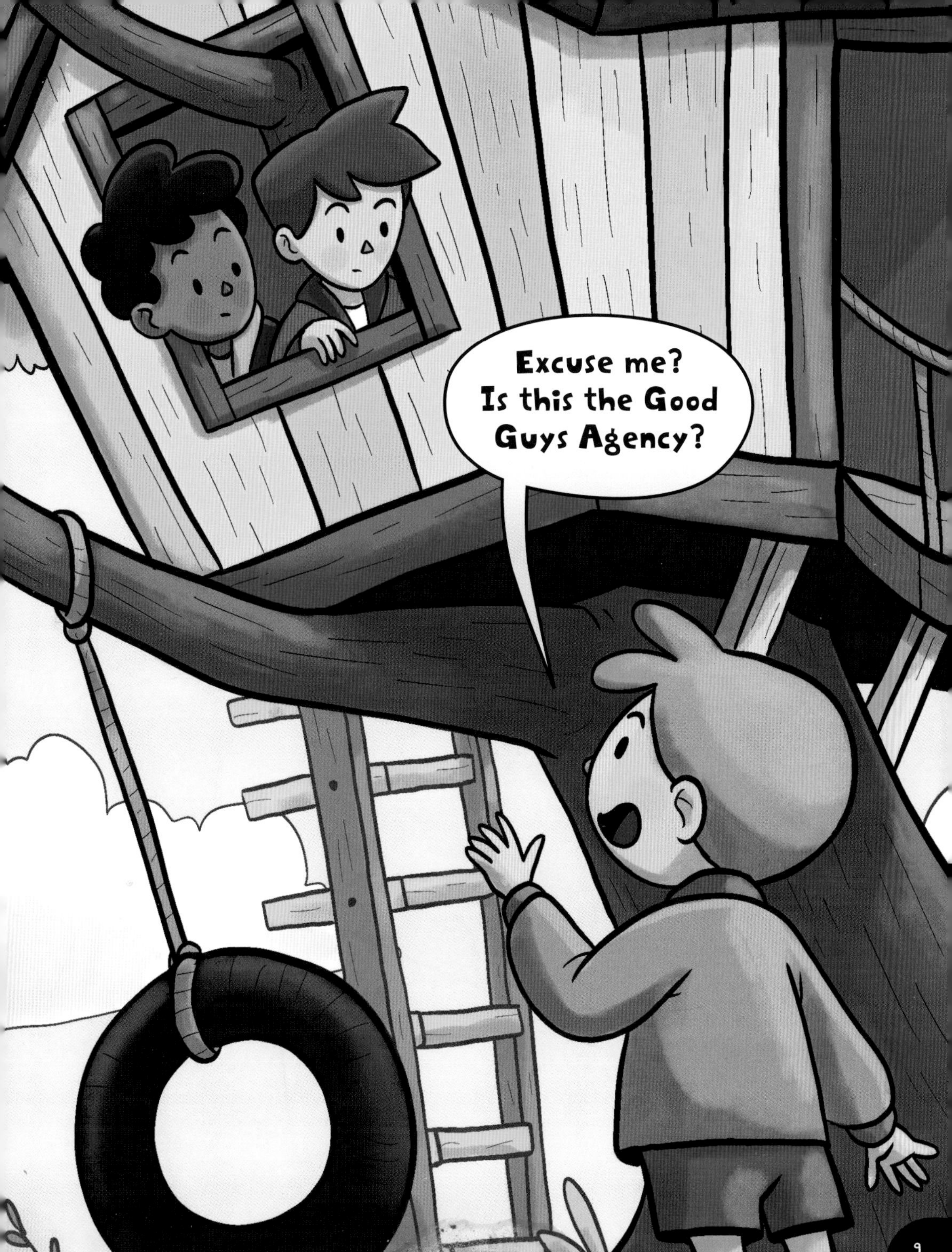
Excuse me? Is this the Good Guys Agency?

"Who are you?" Lucky asked, his voice suspicious. "And how do you know about the Good Guys Agency? We just decided on the name two seconds ago."

"I'm Red, and I just moved in next door, and, well, you were talking pretty loudly."

Rudy nodded in agreement, as Lucky rarely spoke quietly. "Did you need something?" he asked.

"I was just looking for kids to play with. I was wondering if . . . I could join the Agency?" Red asked hopefully.

"Just one moment, please," said Rudy. He and Lucky disappeared into the clubhouse.

"This could be perfect," said Lucky. "With Red, we would have enough people to actually *be* an agency!"

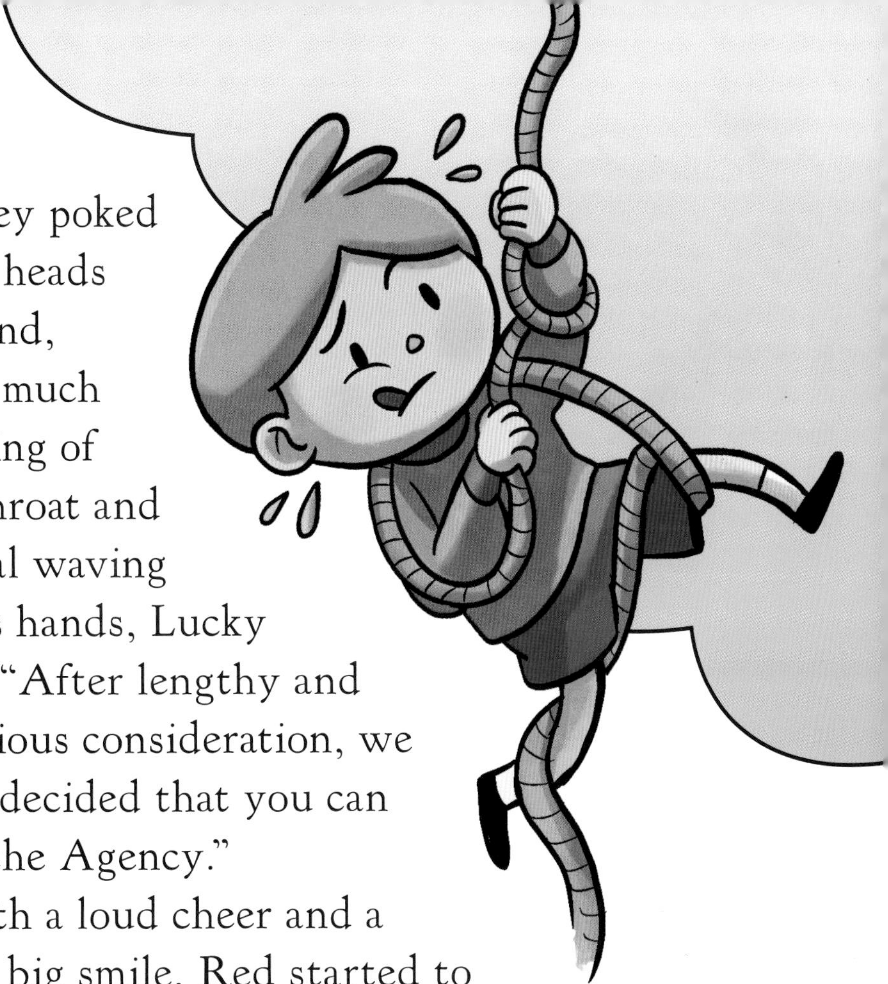

They poked their heads out and, with much clearing of his throat and formal waving of his hands, Lucky said, "After lengthy and judicious consideration, we have decided that you can join the Agency."

With a loud cheer and a great big smile, Red started to climb the rope that dangled from the top floor of the treehouse. There was much grunting and puffing, and Red's face finally appeared through the hole in the floor.

"You know, next time, you could use the

ladder," Lucky said. But Red just collapsed onto the floor in a heap of exhaustion.

"So. . ." he panted, "what is . . . this club . . . all about . . . anyway?"

Lucky jumped back onto his soapbox, and Rudy rolled his eyes. "Oh brother, you had to ask."

"Like many great ideas, our agency started in a garage," Lucky intoned. "Then Mom came home from work and needed to park her car, so we were banished to the backyard. But though our clubhouse has changed, our dream has remained the same. Now, Red, you may be

asking yourself, 'What do we *do* at the Good Guys Agency?'"

"I know, I just asked that," Red said, but Lucky plowed on.

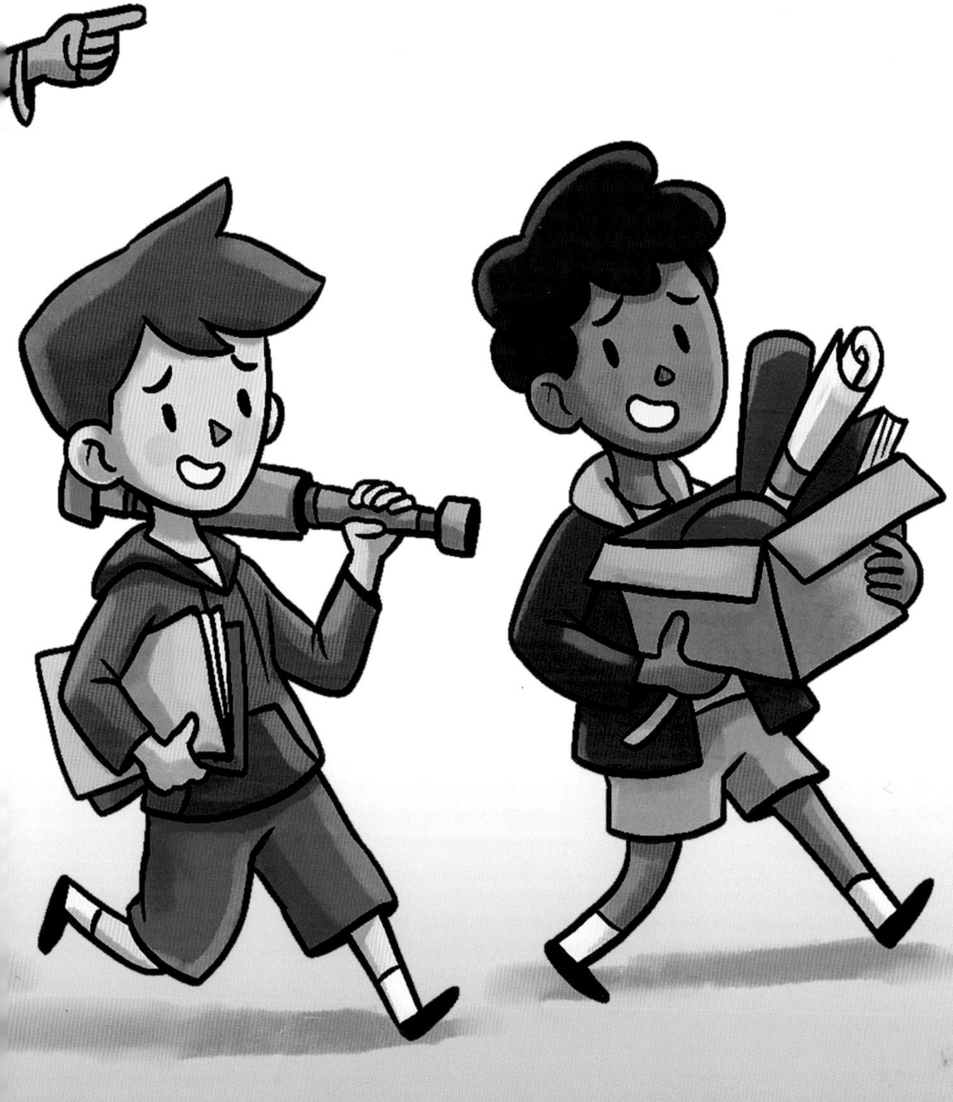

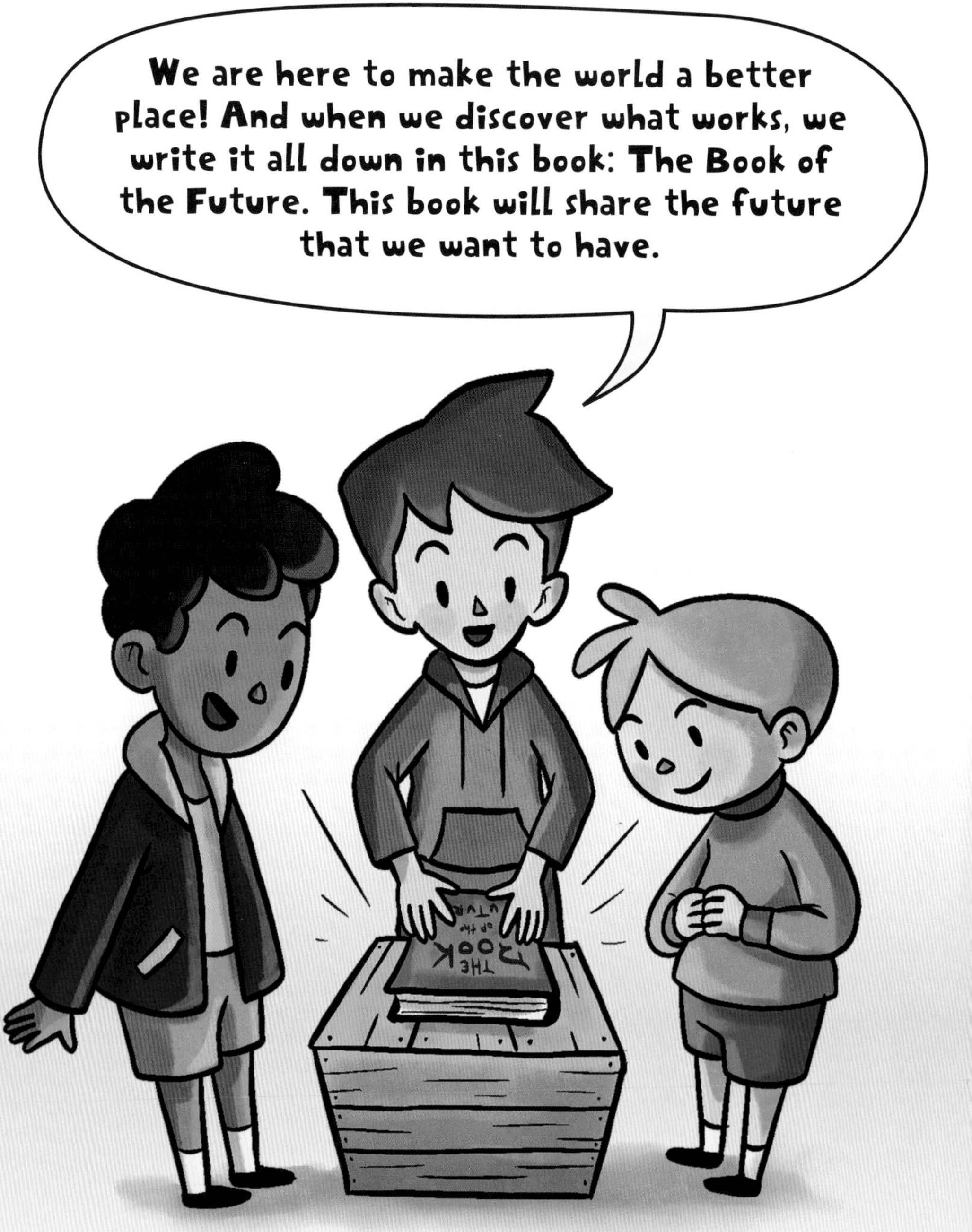
We are here to make the world a better place! And when we discover what works, we write it all down in this book: The Book of the Future. This book will share the future that we want to have.

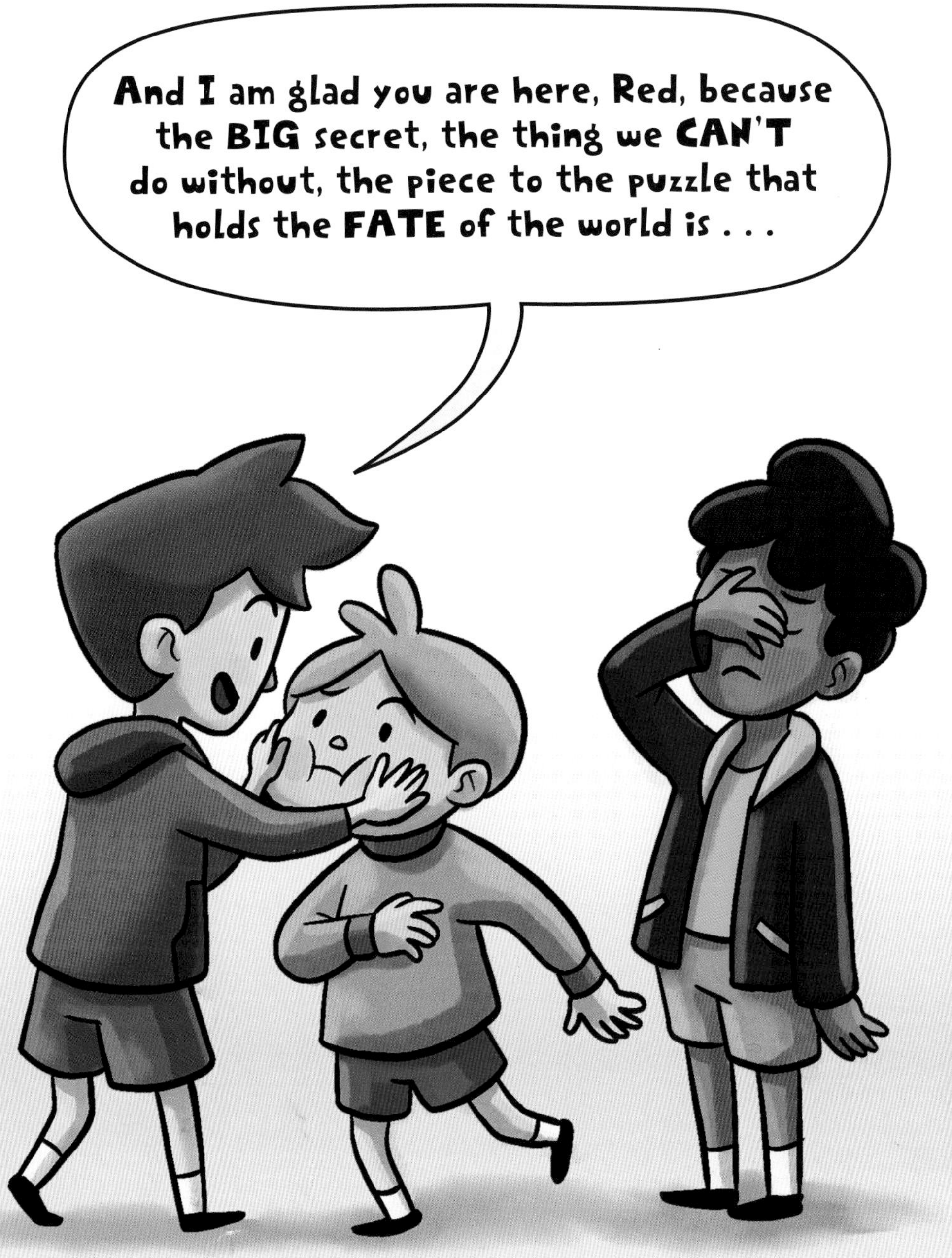
And I am glad you are here, Red, because the BIG secret, the thing we CAN'T do without, the piece to the puzzle that holds the FATE of the world is . . .

Aaaa wooo gaaa!

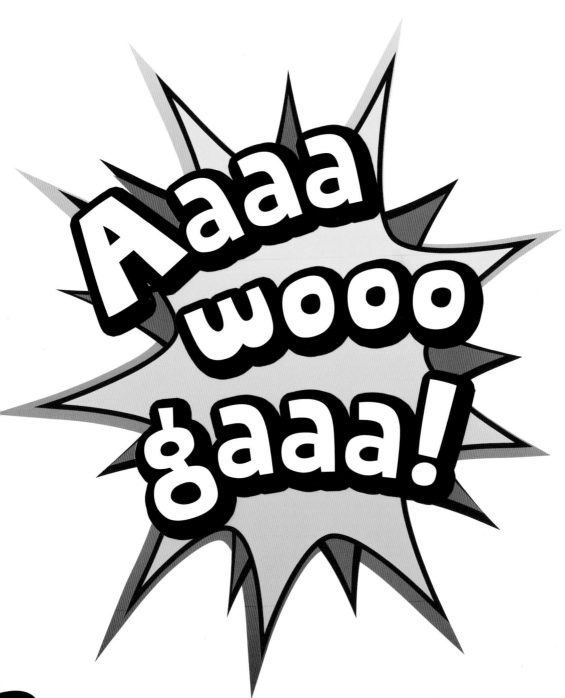

"Wait! No time to talk," Lucky said. "That's the siren—we have to go! We have a new case." He grabbed the rope and swung to the ground.

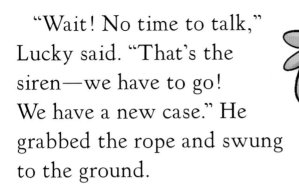

Aaaawooogaa!

"But the thing! What's the one thing?!" Red tried to ask as he, too—somewhat less enthusiastically—inched down the rope.

Aaaawooogaa!

But Lucky was already sprinting across the grass.

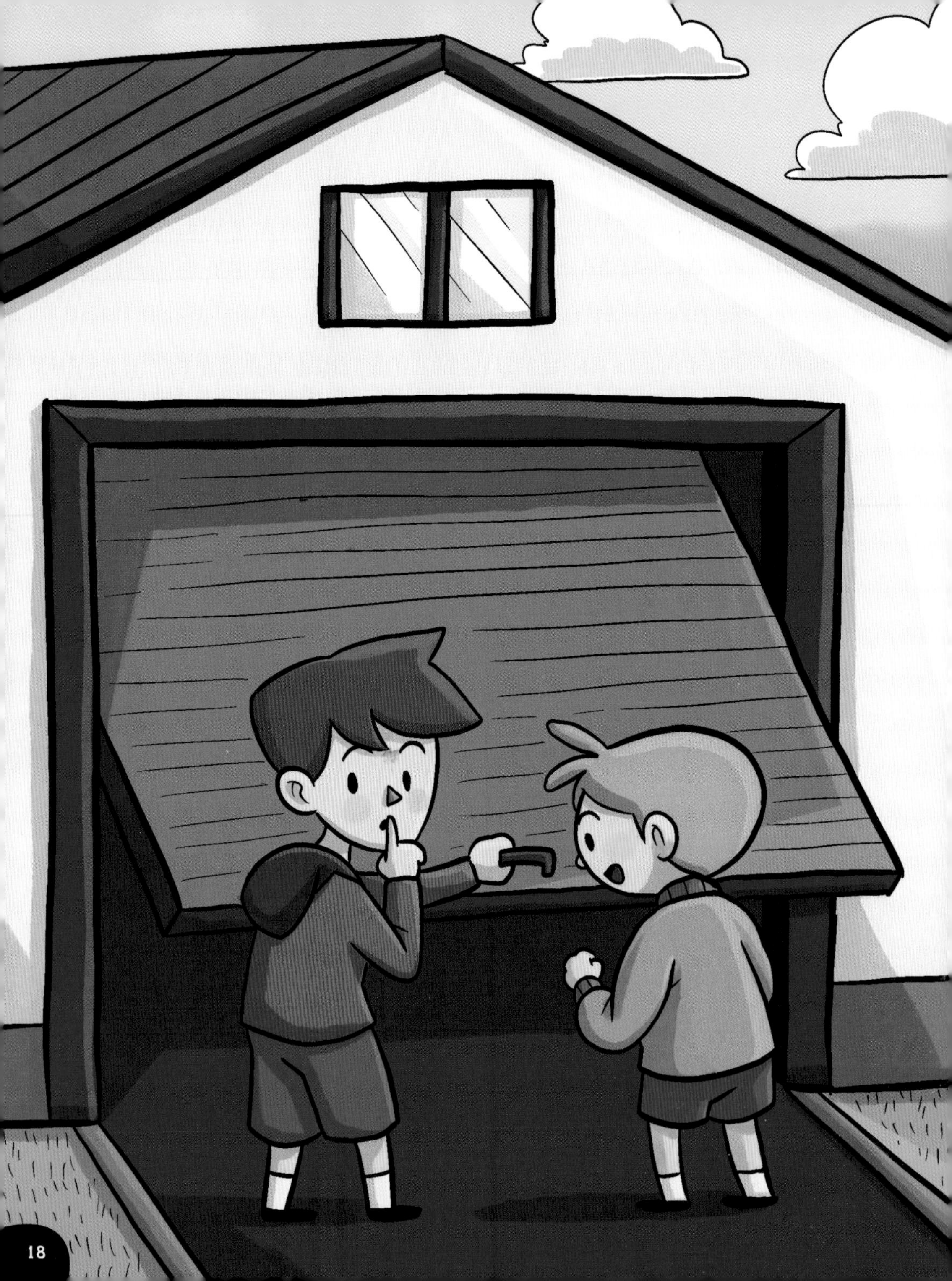

CHAPTER TWO

Trouble at Fort Crumble

"Everyone, get to your positions!" Lucky shouted as he ran. "Rudy, you head to the clubhouse library, while Red and I get on the road."

"The road?! Where are we going?" Red panted.

Lucky seized Red by the hand and led him to the garage, which, though it couldn't hold a clubhouse, was the perfect fit for something else.

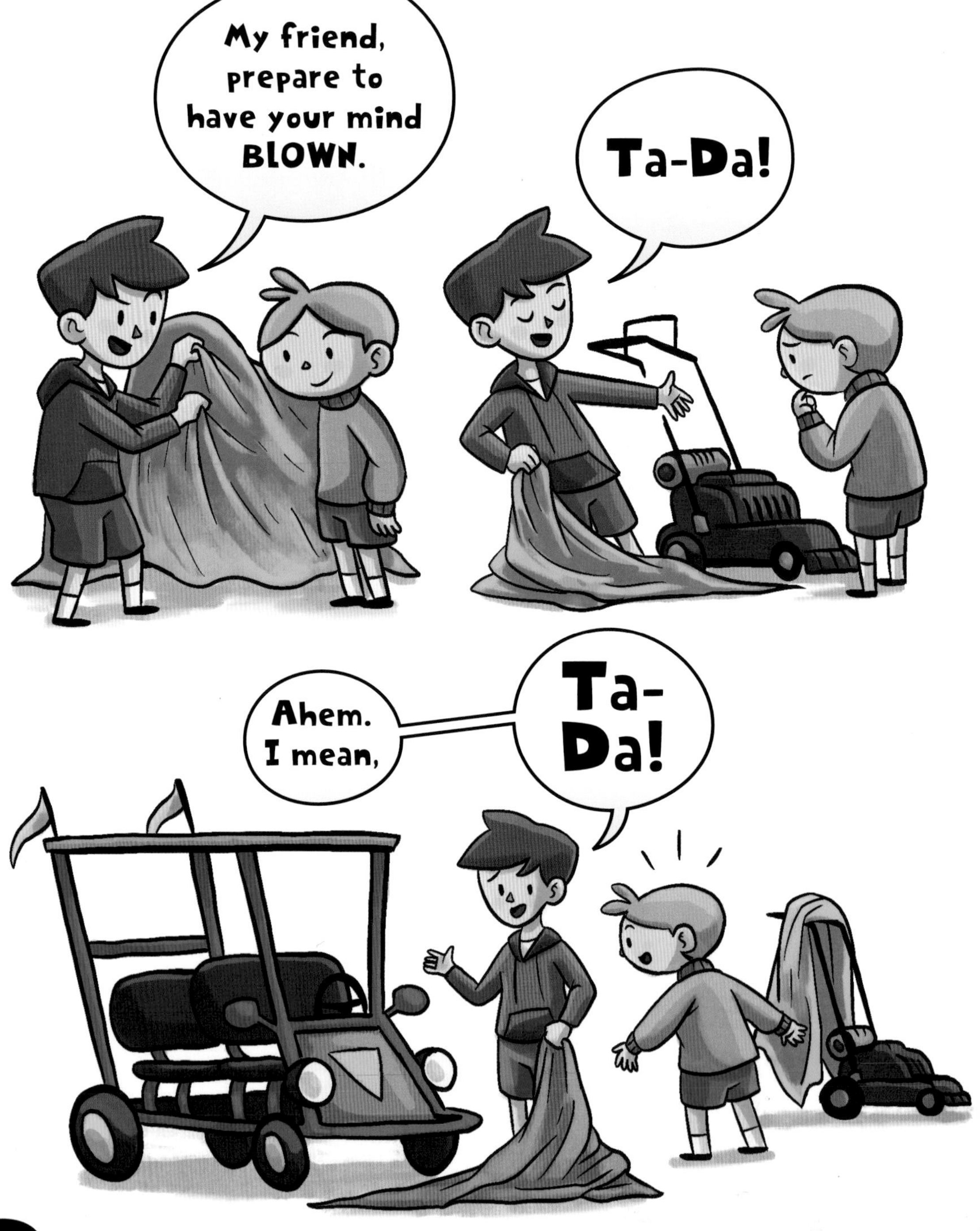
My friend, prepare to have your mind BLOWN.
Ta-Da!
Ahem. I mean,
Ta-Da!

"What is *this*?" asked Red. The day had just gotten much more exciting.

"This is the Kid Cruiser! Come on, get in. I'm driving." Lucky jumped into the driver's side of the car. "There's no time to lose!"

Red clambered into the passenger seat.

"Okay, everyone ready?" Lucky shouted.

Red looked around and realized he *was* everyone. "Ready!" he said.

"Repeat after me: Heads high! Feet down low! Everyone ready! Here we go!" Lucky said, and the Kid Cruiser was off.

"Hurry, Red, turn on the siren," Lucky shouted over the sound of the wind.

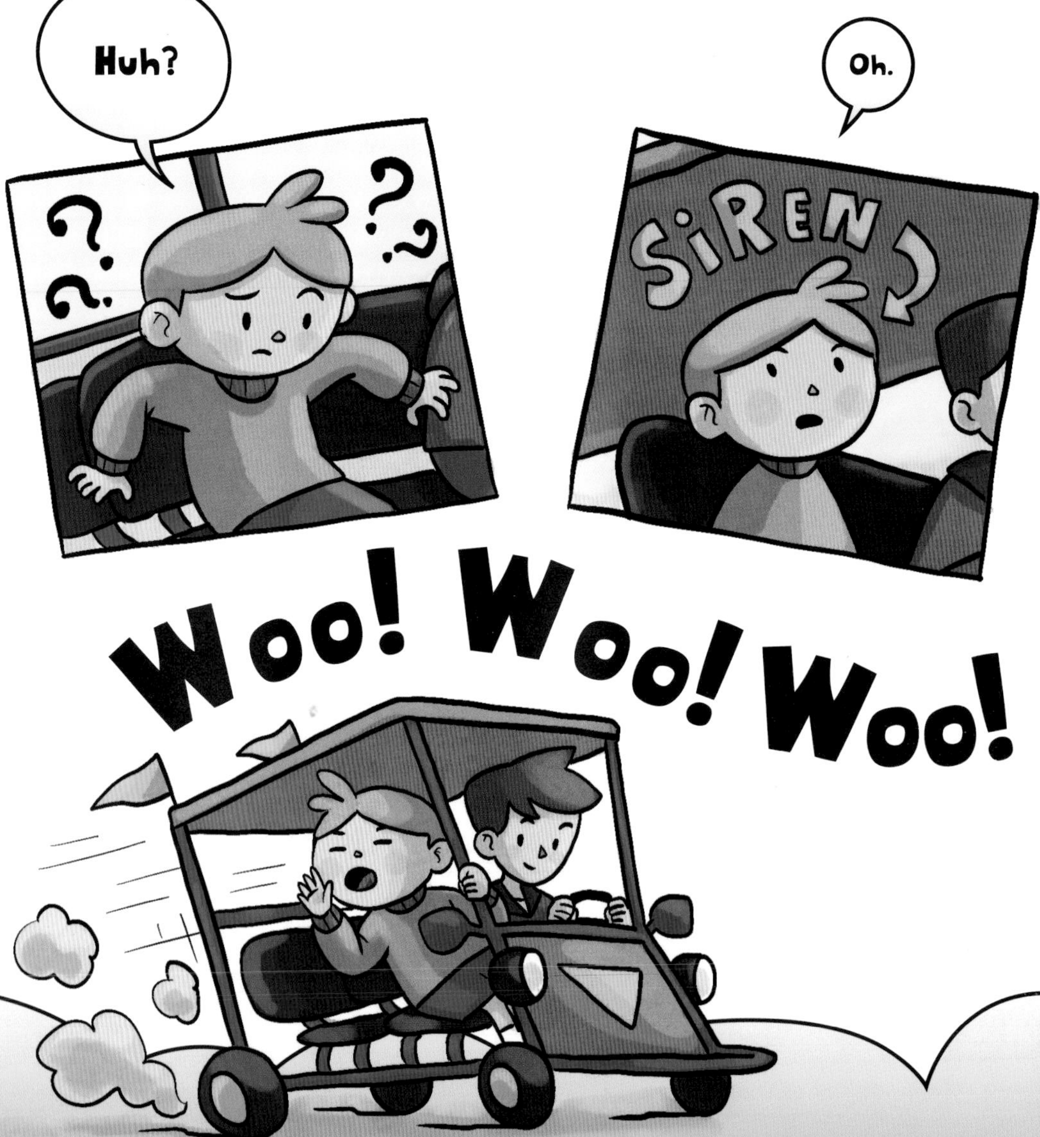
Huh?
Oh.
SIREN
Woo! Woo! Woo!

The two of them cruised from Lucky's house all the way to Fort Crumble, which, it turned out, was most perfectly named. In the middle of a cloud of dust was a pile of wood, and in the middle of that pile was a boy, and on the boy's face was a terrific scowl.

"We're the Good Guys Agency. What seems to be the problem?" Lucky said, pulling out his badge.

"Lucky, it's me, Charlie from school," Charlie said. "And *that* is a library card."

"Of course not," said Lucky. "Now, what seems to be the problem?"

"My fort fell down again! This is the fifth time!"

That's why we call it **Fort Crumble.**

"It was all my little brother Teddy's fault," Charlie continued. "I have been building it all day! He's always trying to hang around me. He ruins things. I want you to arrest him!"

"Charlie, we don't arrest people," Lucky corrected him.

"But you have a siren," Charlie responded.

"We *do* have a siren," Red agreed.

"Where is Teddy now?" asked Lucky.

"He ran inside crying. I yelled at him after he knocked the fort down."

Lucky jumped onto the pile of rubble, put his hands on his hips, looked into the distance, and proclaimed, "This is a job for the Good Guys Agency!"

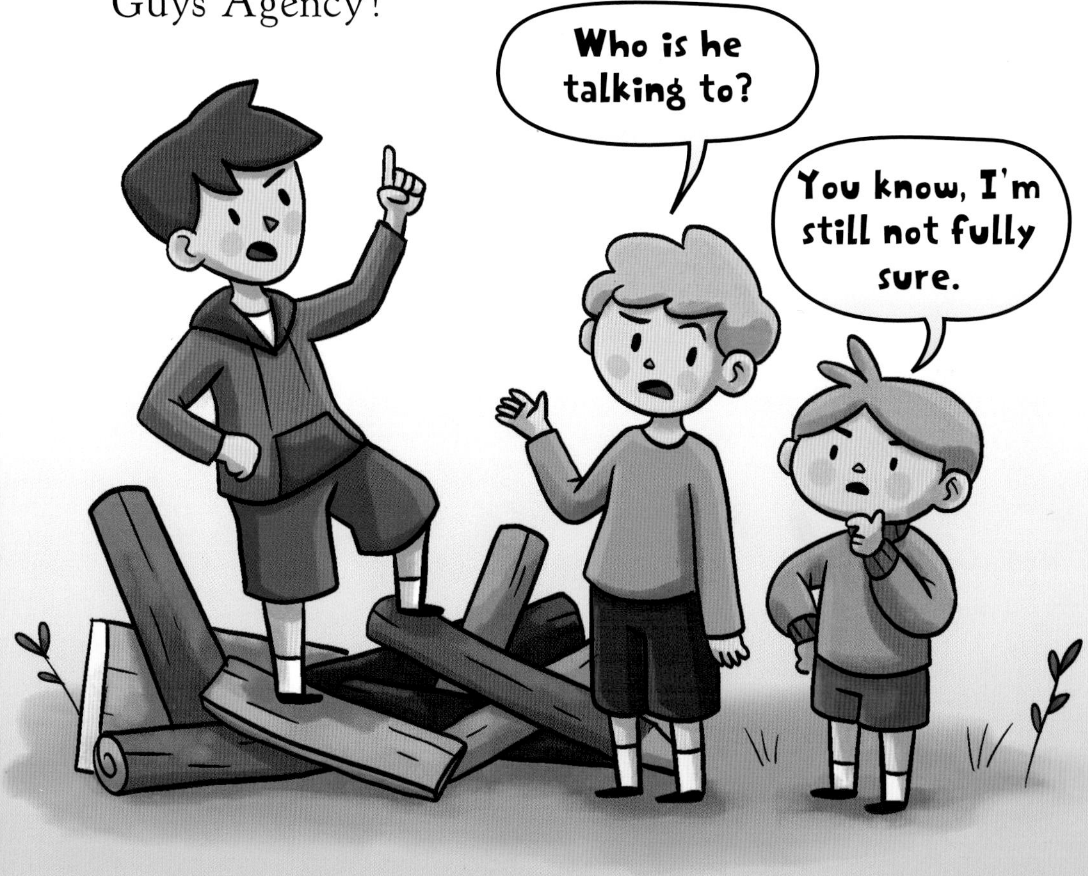
Who is he talking to?
You know, I'm still not fully sure.

"Everyone, get in the Kid Cruiser," Lucky instructed. "It's time to go to Imagination Station!"

Lucky grabbed a metal can that was connected to a string attached to the cruiser.

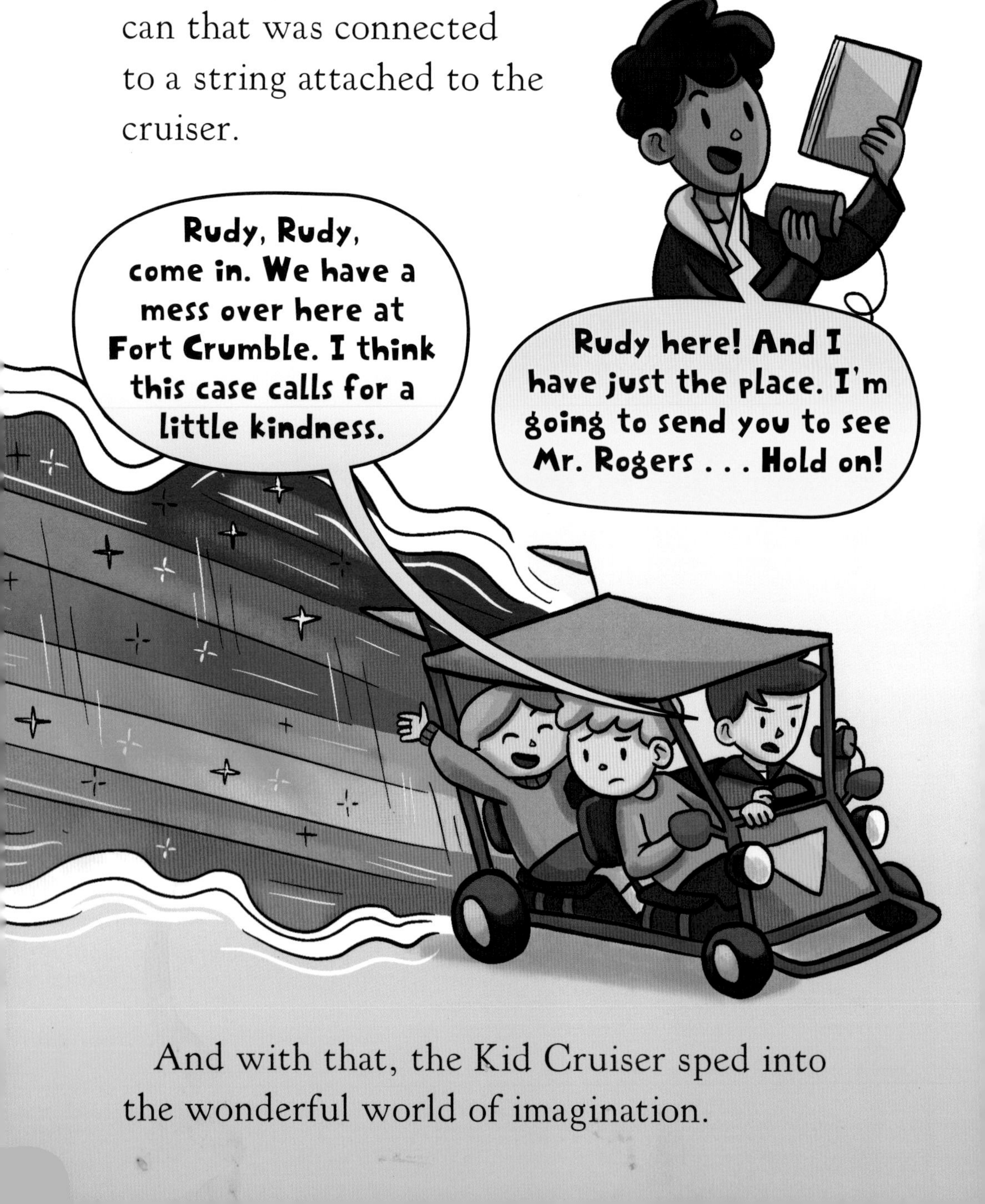
Rudy, Rudy, come in. We have a mess over here at Fort Crumble. I think this case calls for a little kindness.
Rudy here! And I have just the place. I'm going to send you to see Mr. Rogers . . . Hold on!

And with that, the Kid Cruiser sped into the wonderful world of imagination.

CHAPTER THREE

Young Freddie

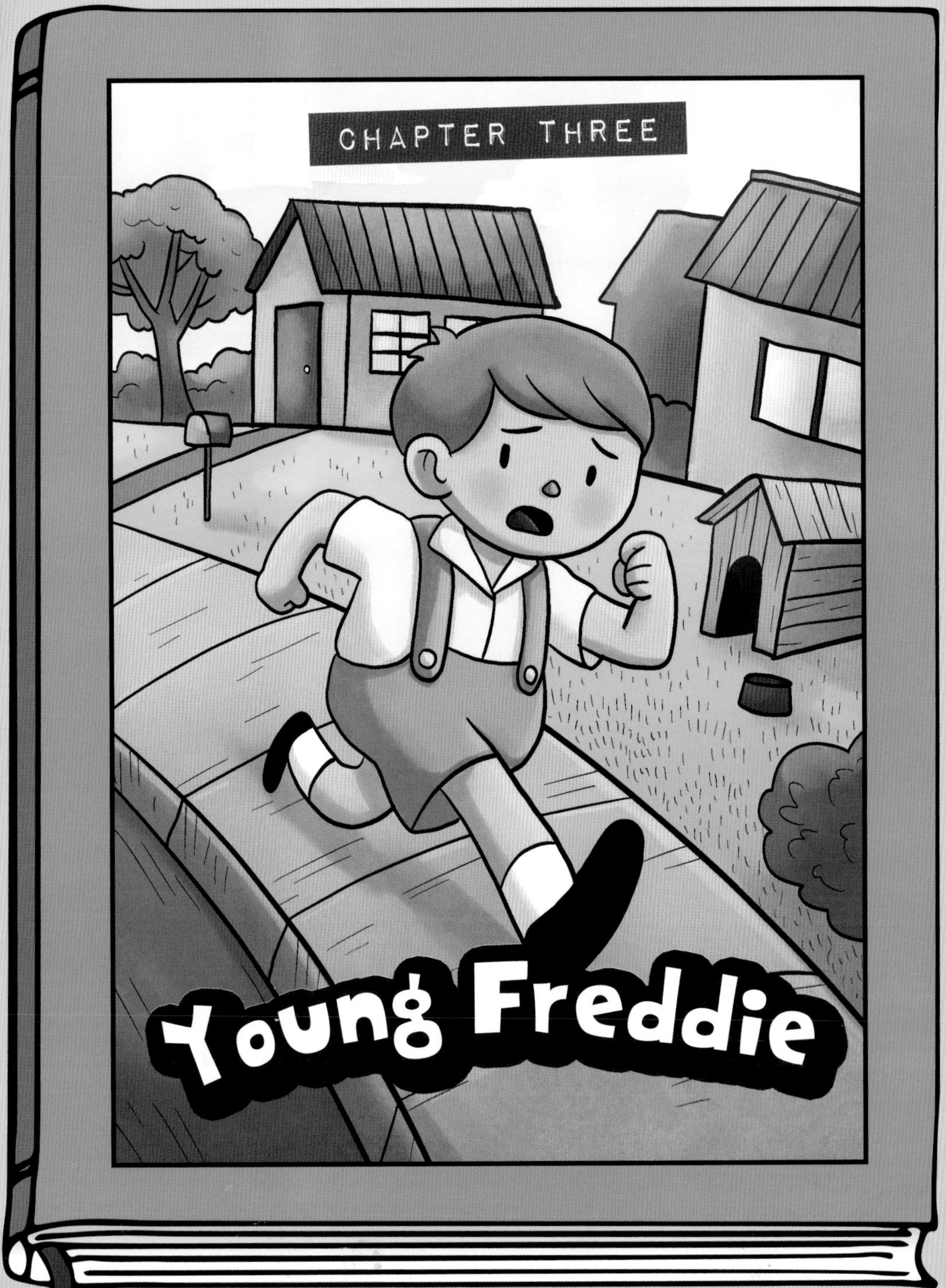

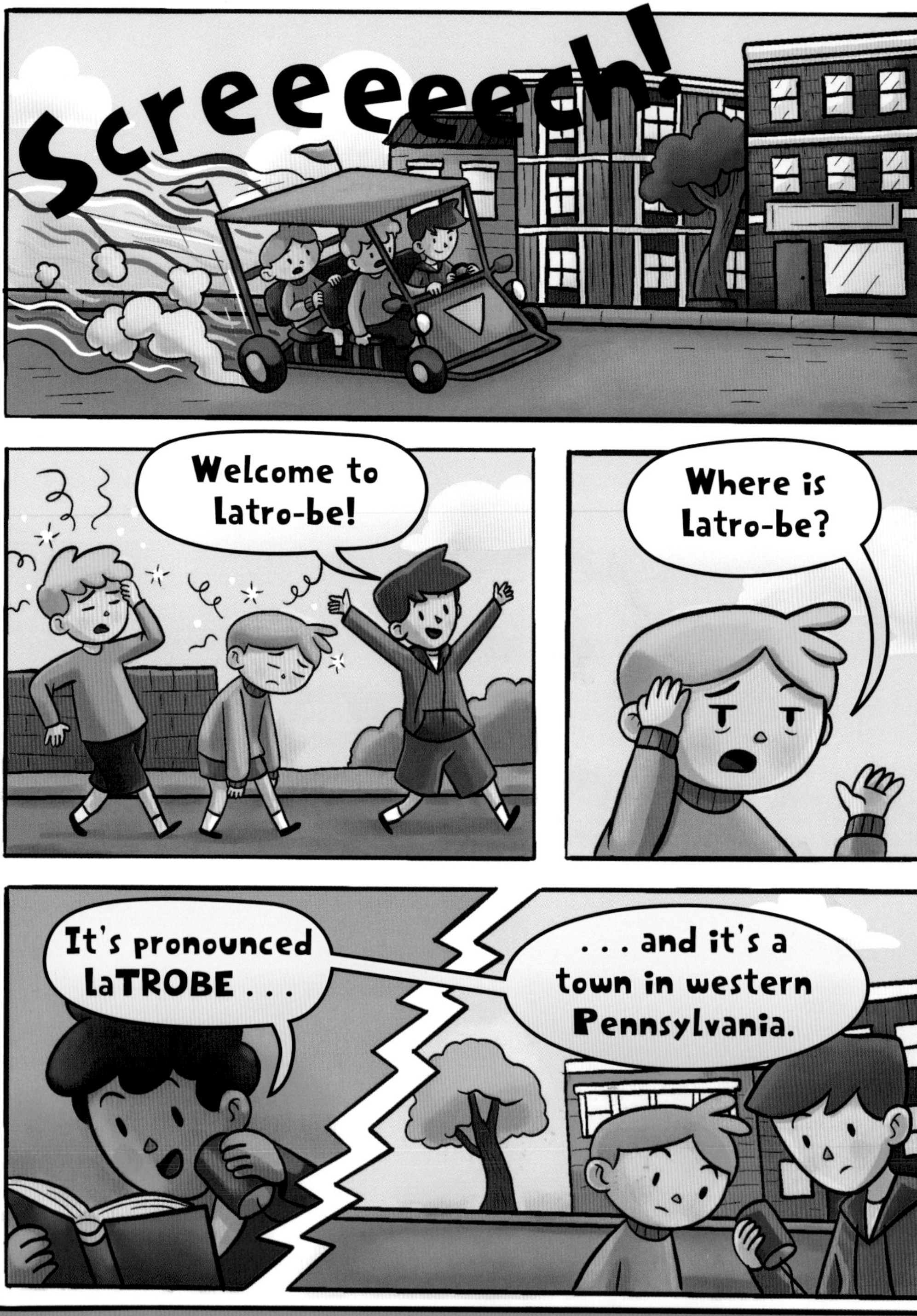
Screeeeech!
Welcome to Latro-be!
Where is Latro-be?
It's pronounced LaTROBE . . .
. . . and it's a town in western Pennsylvania.

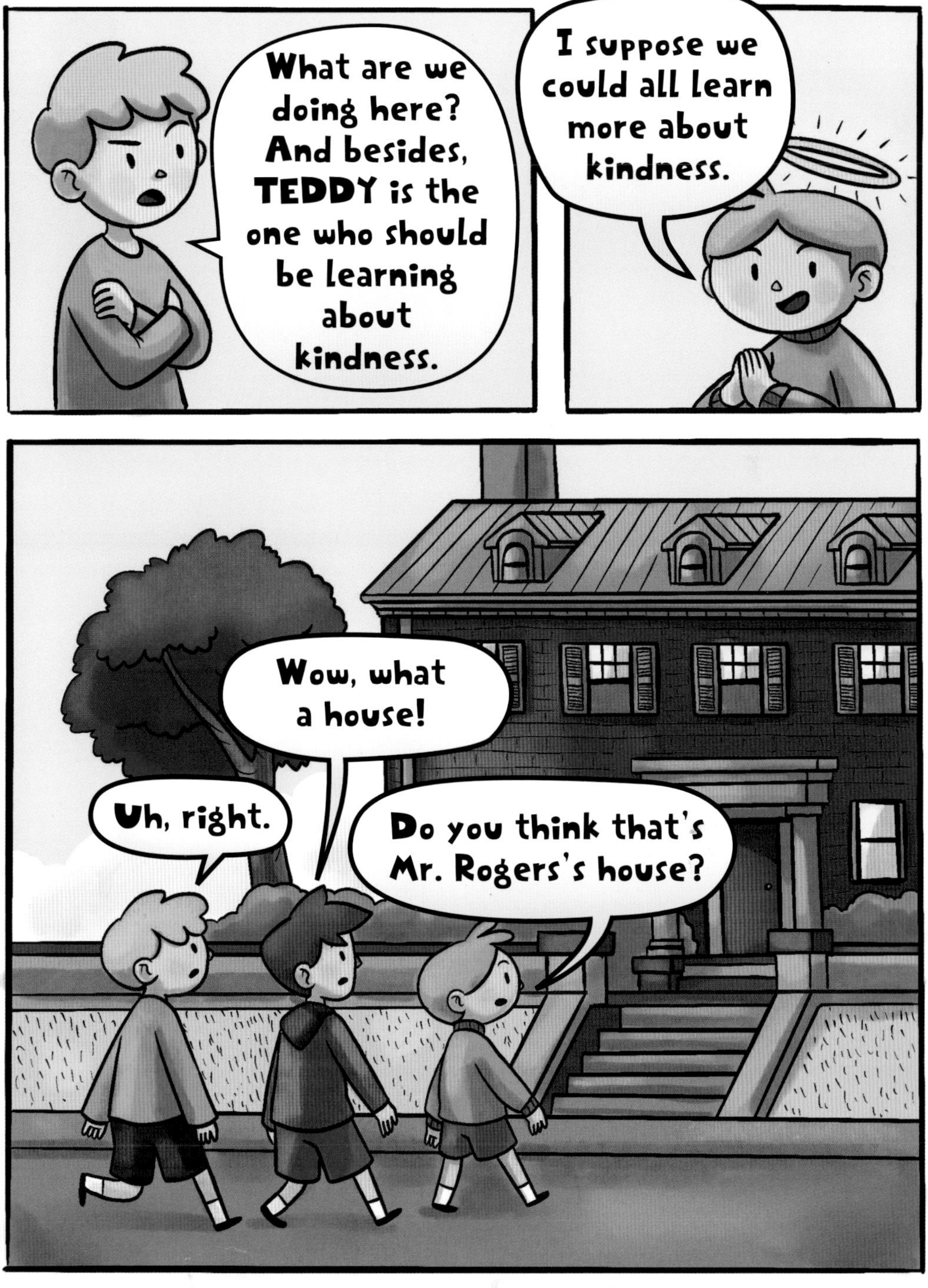
What are we doing here? And besides, TEDDY is the one who should be learning about kindness.
I suppose we could all learn more about kindness.
Wow, what a house!
Uh, right.
Do you think that's Mr. Rogers's house?

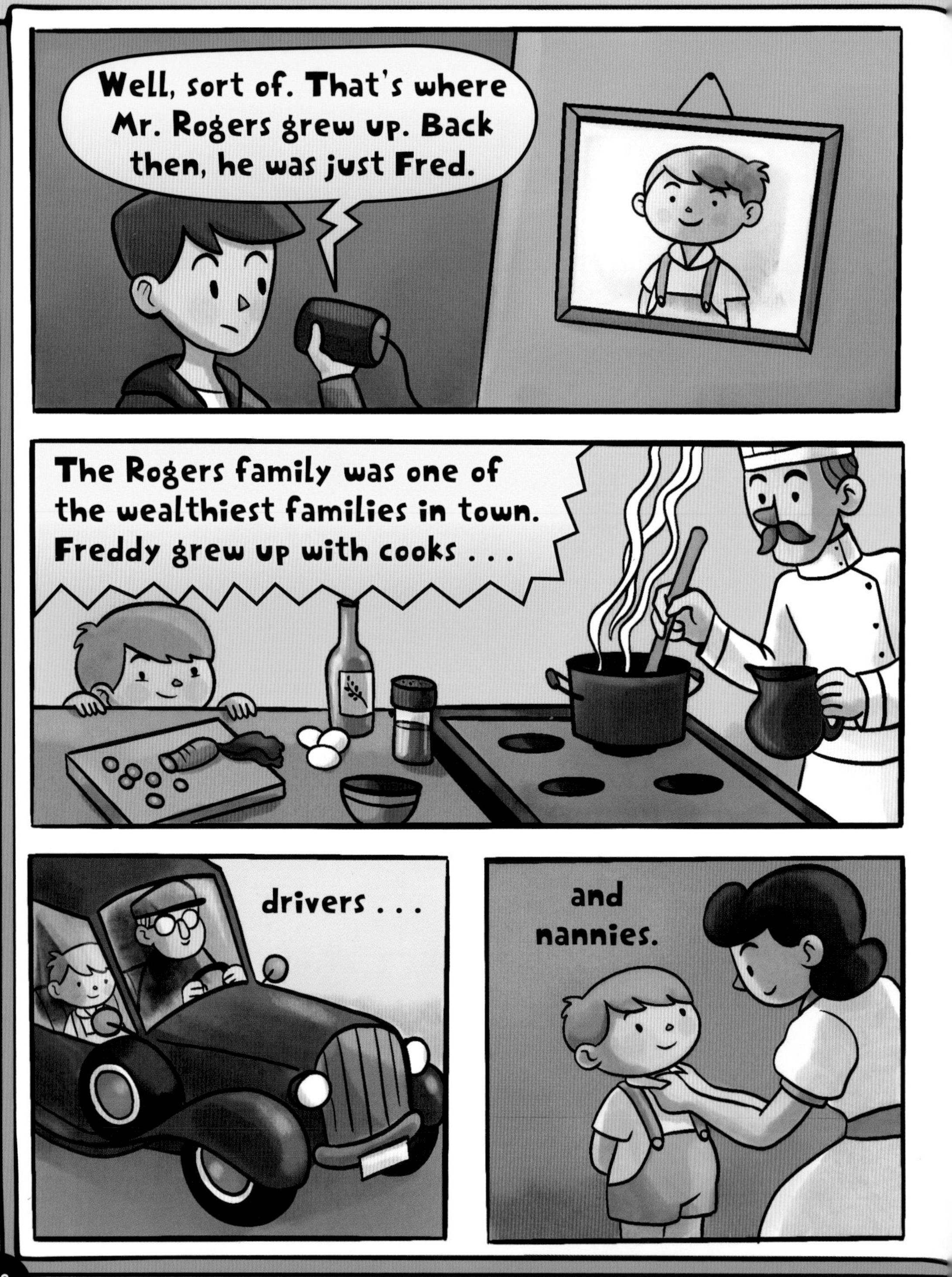
Well, sort of. That's where Mr. Rogers grew up. Back then, he was just Fred.
The Rogers family was one of the wealthiest families in town. Freddy grew up with cooks . . .
drivers . . .
and nannies.

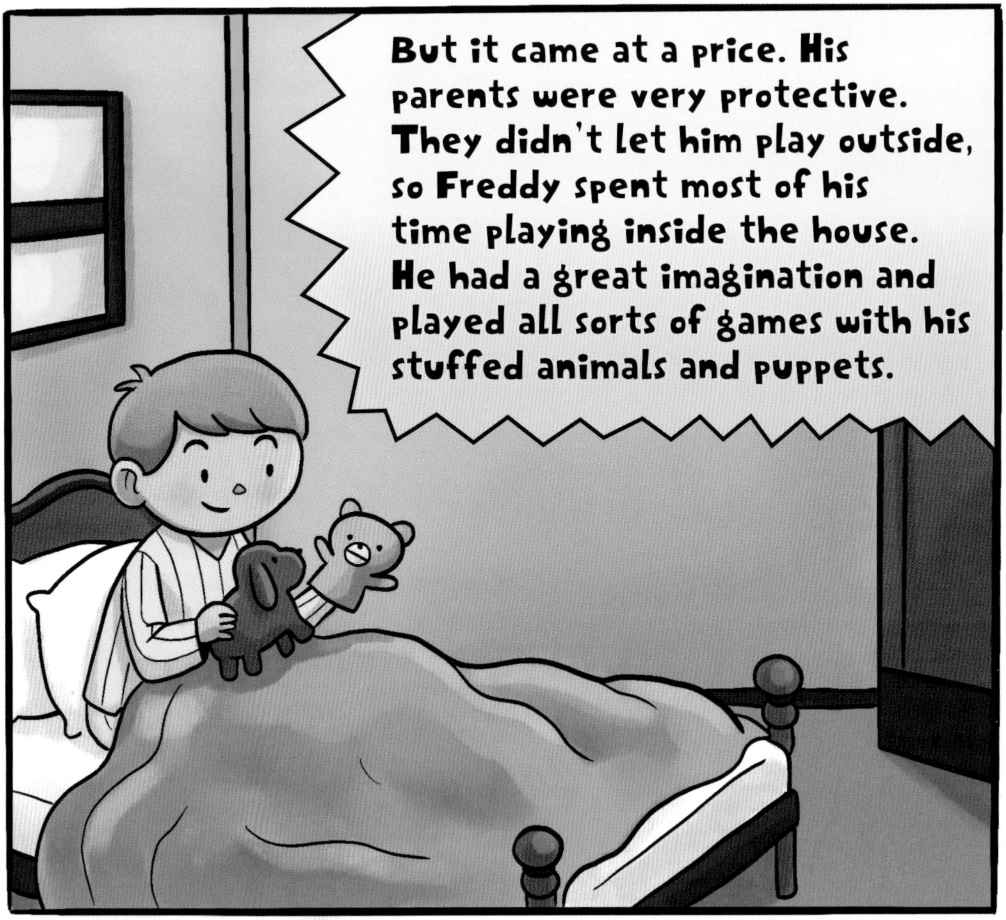
But it came at a price. His parents were very protective. They didn't let him play outside, so Freddy spent most of his time playing inside the house. He had a great imagination and played all sorts of games with his stuffed animals and puppets.

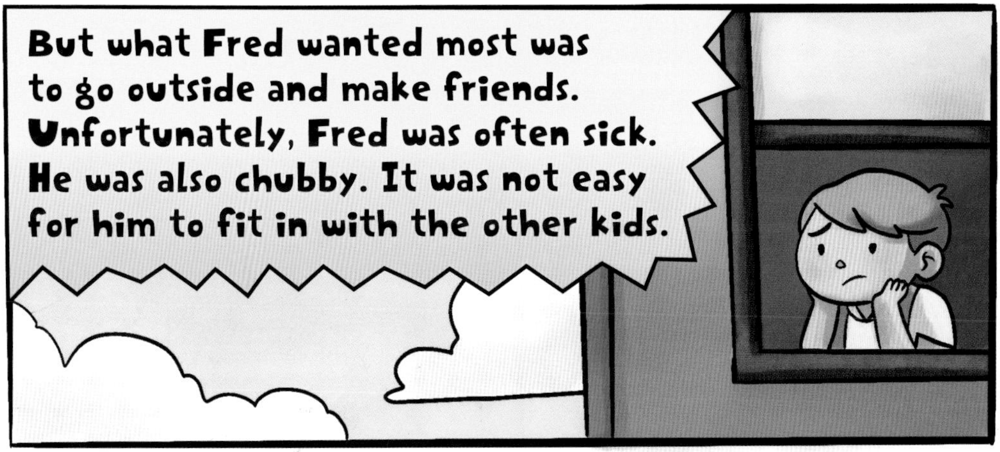
But what Fred wanted most was to go outside and make friends. Unfortunately, Fred was often sick. He was also chubby. It was not easy for him to fit in with the other kids.

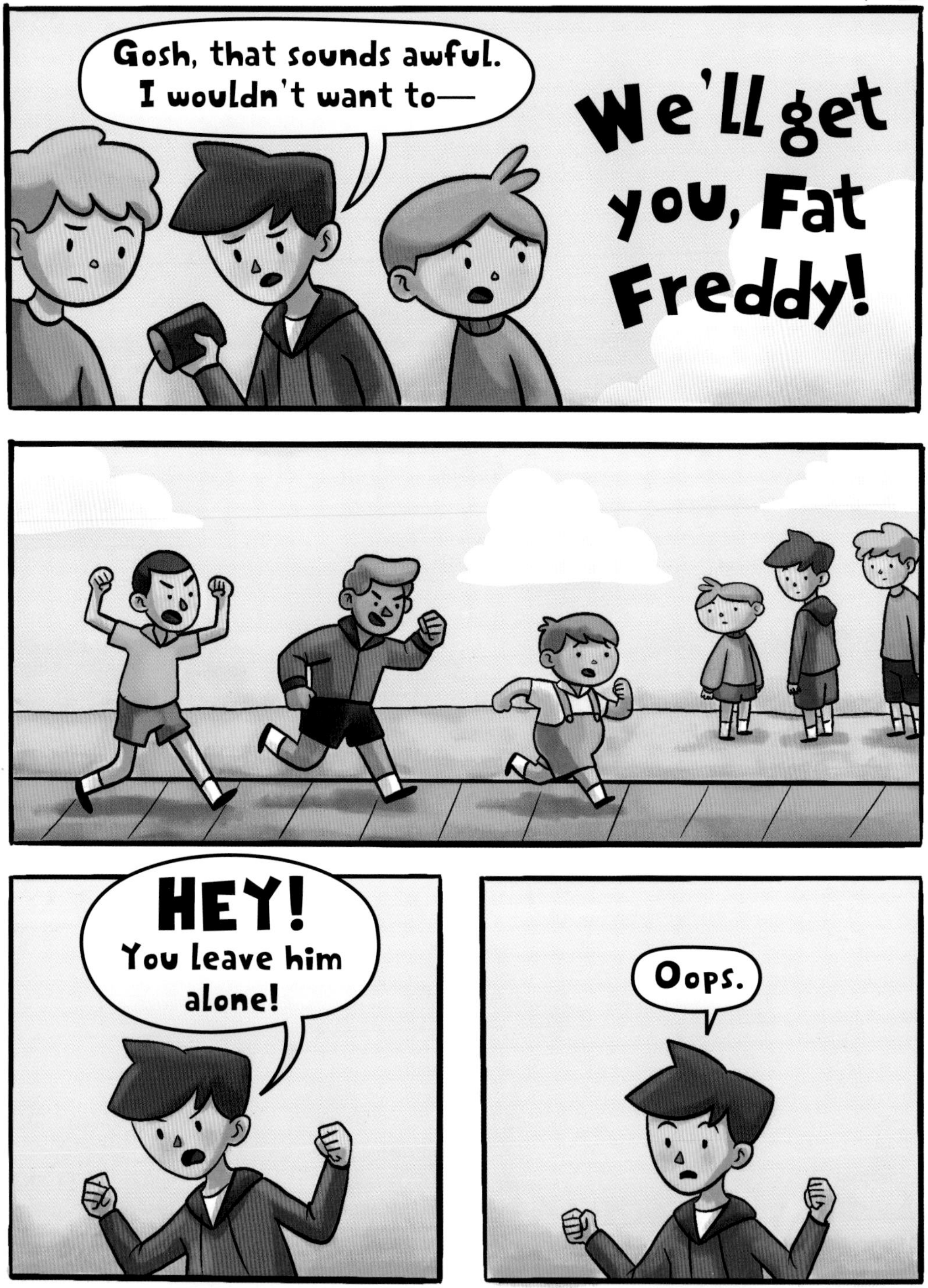

Gosh, that sounds awful. I wouldn't want to—
We'll get you, Fat Freddy!
HEY! You leave him alone!
Oops.

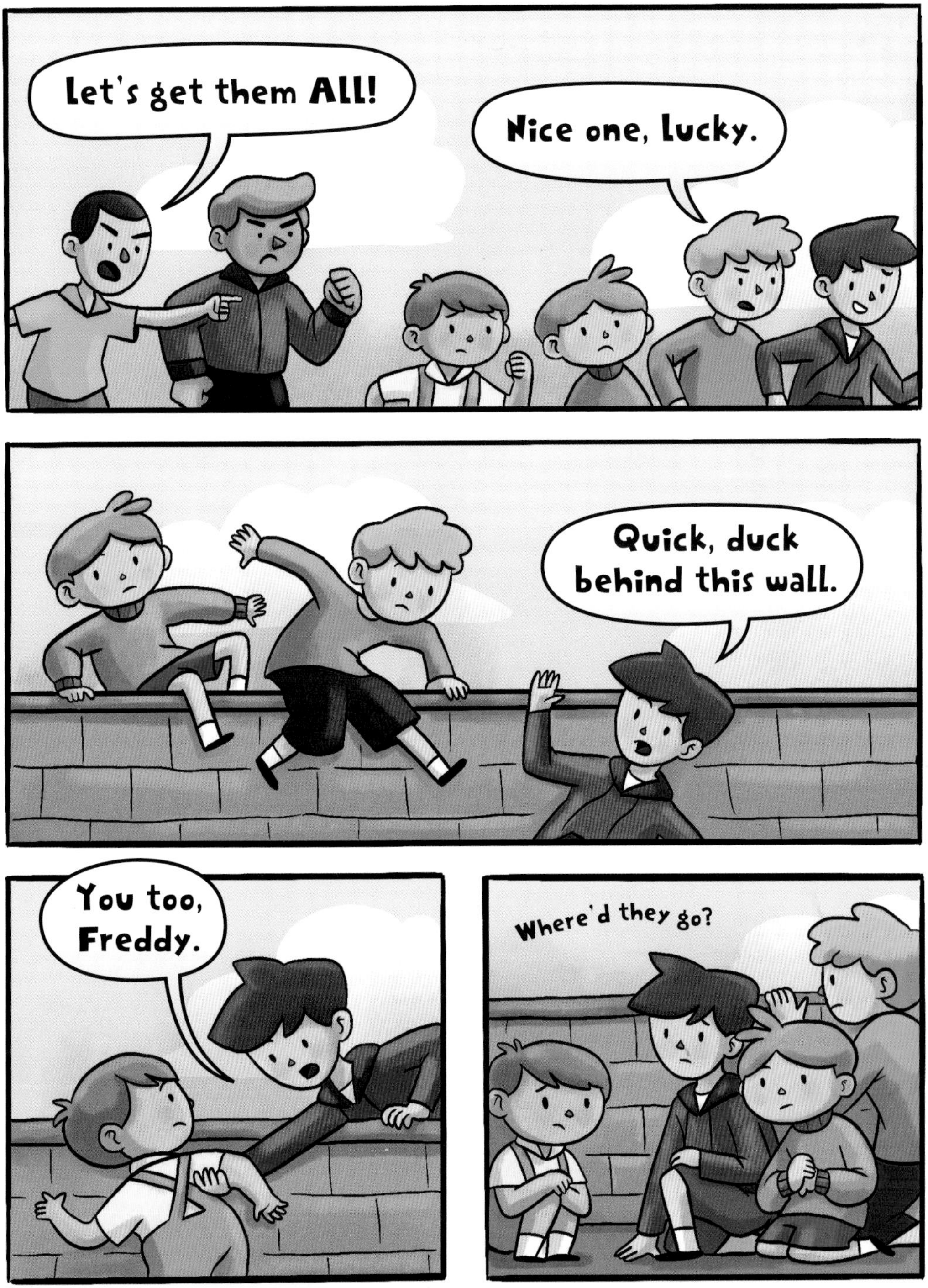

Let's get them ALL!
Nice one, Lucky.
Quick, duck behind this wall.
You too, Freddy.
Where'd they go?

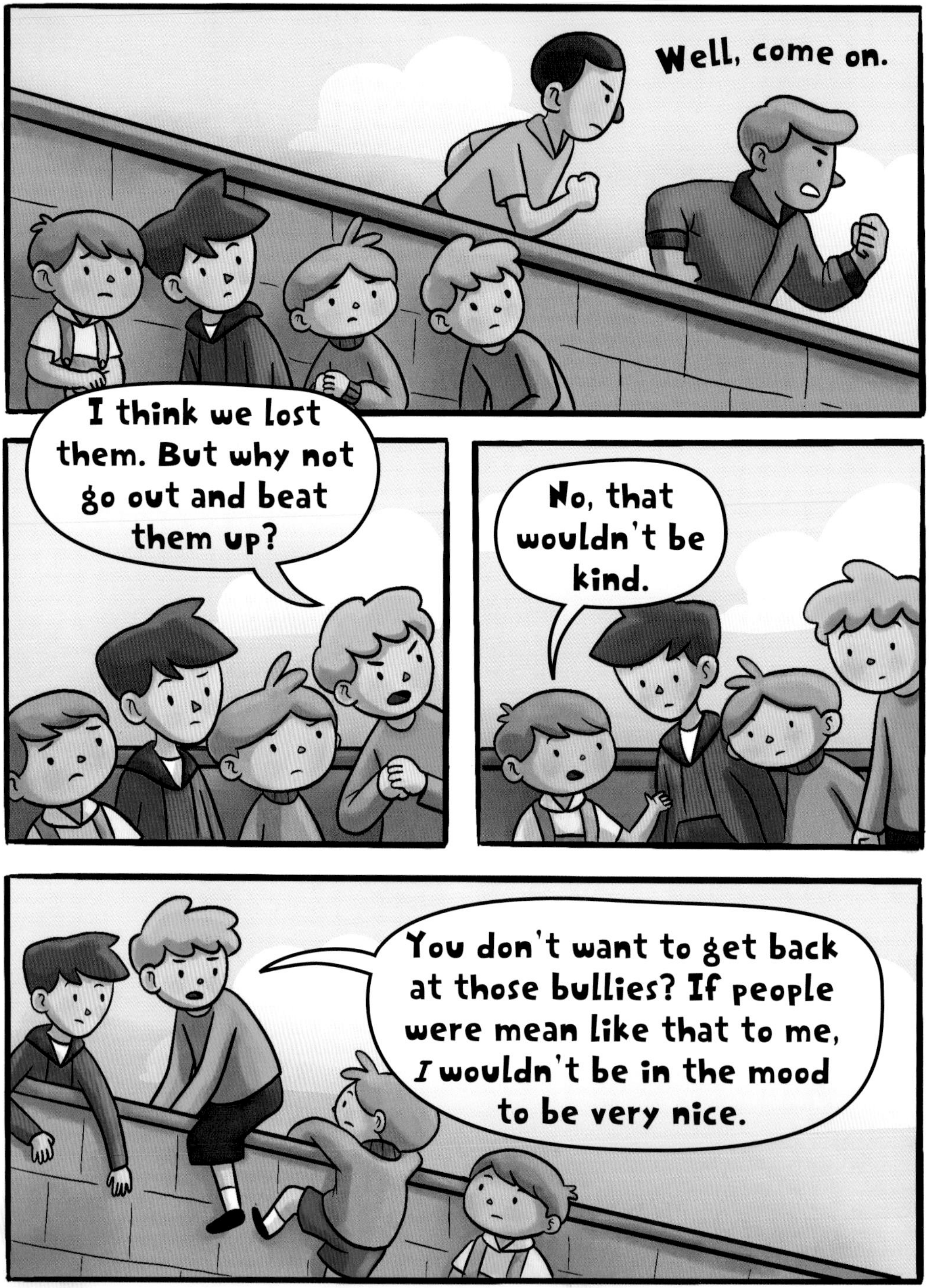
Well, come on.
I think we lost them. But why not go out and beat them up?
No, that wouldn't be kind.
You don't want to get back at those bullies? If people were mean like that to me, *I* wouldn't be in the mood to be very nice.

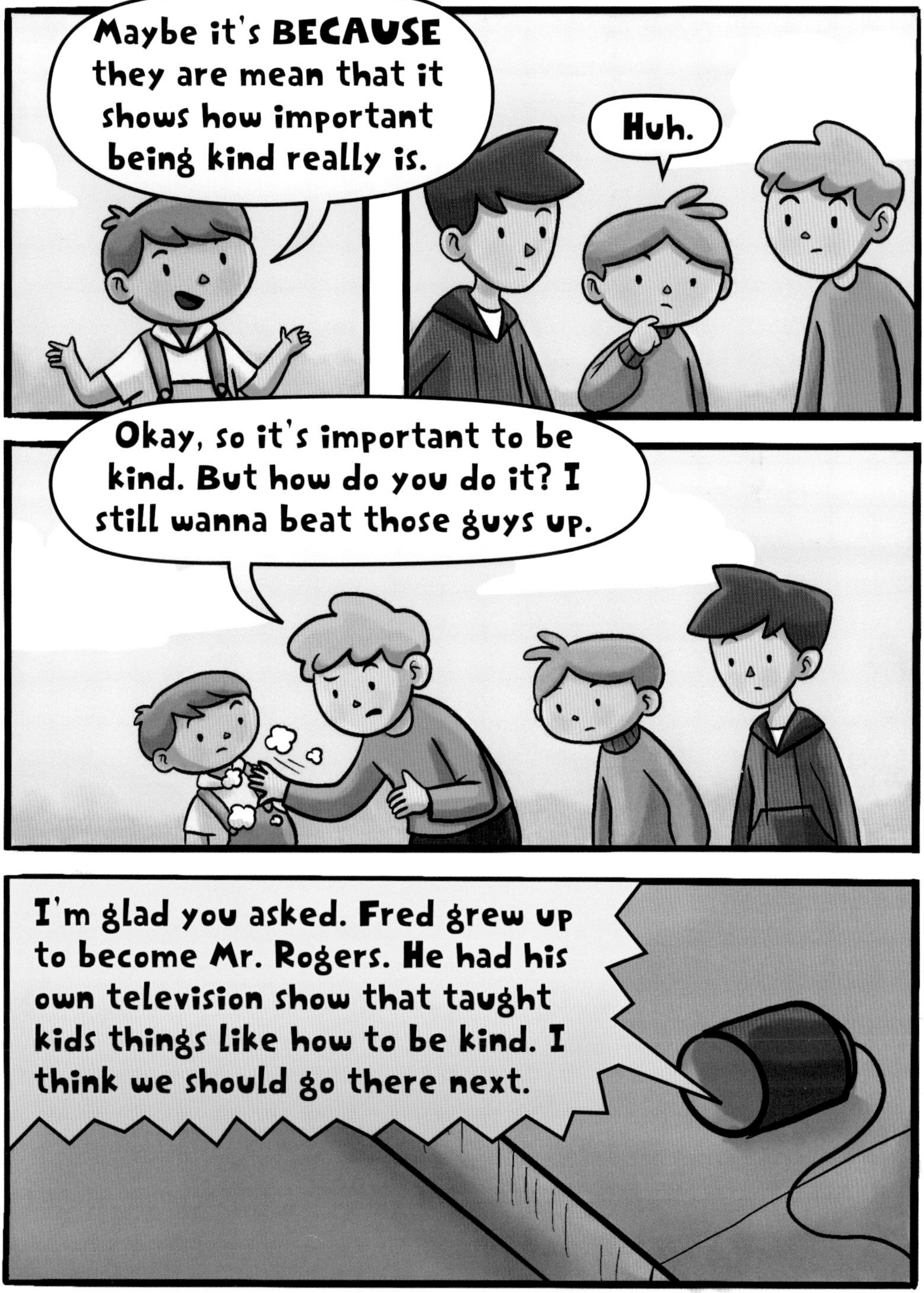
Maybe it's BECAUSE they are mean that it shows how important being kind really is.
Huh.
Okay, so it's important to be kind. But how do you do it? I still wanna beat those guys up.
I'm glad you asked. Fred grew up to become Mr. Rogers. He had his own television show that taught kids things like how to be kind. I think we should go there next.

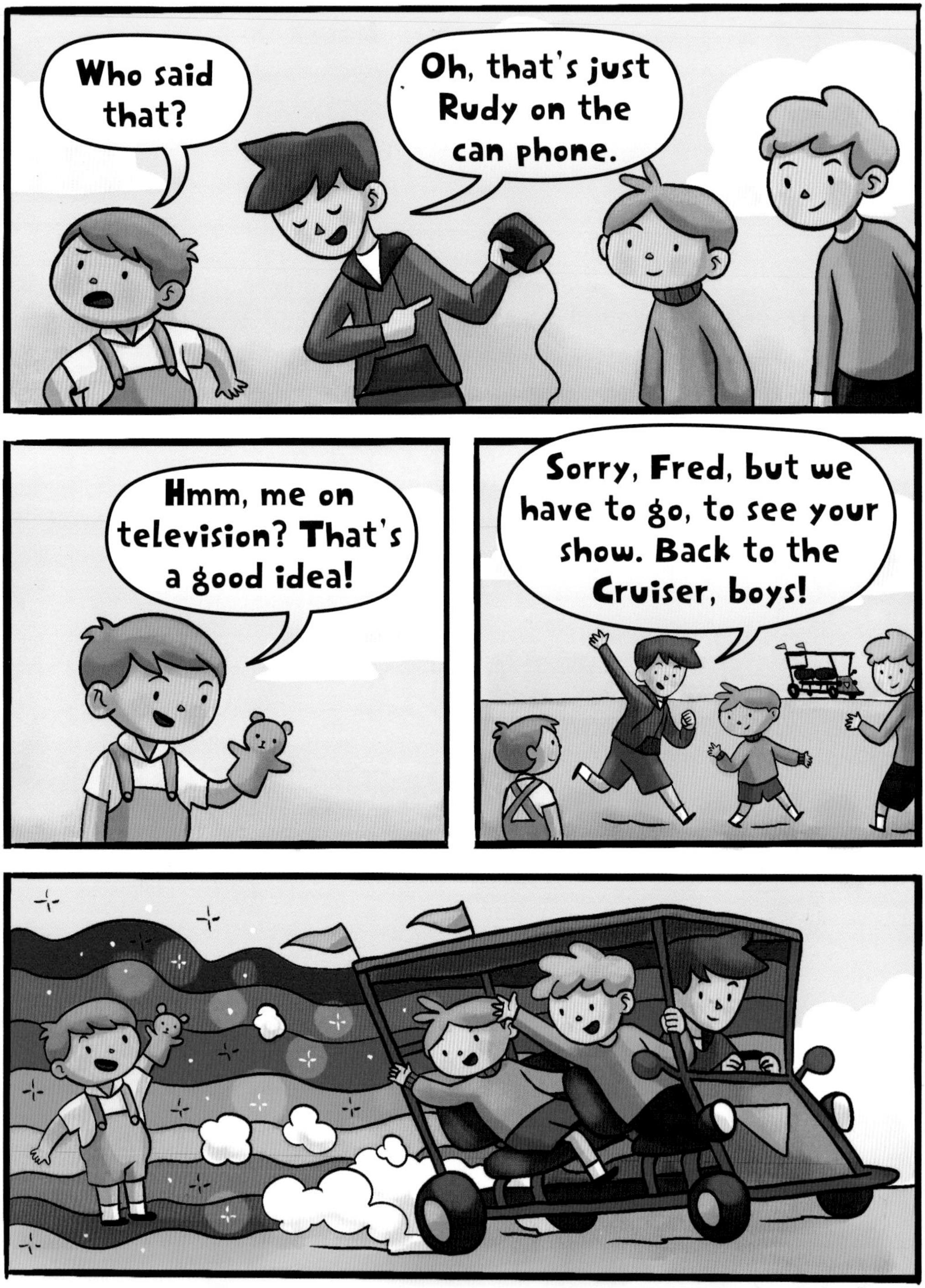
Who said that?
Oh, that's just Rudy on the can phone.
Hmm, me on television? That's a good idea!
Sorry, Fred, but we have to go, to see your show. Back to the Cruiser, boys!

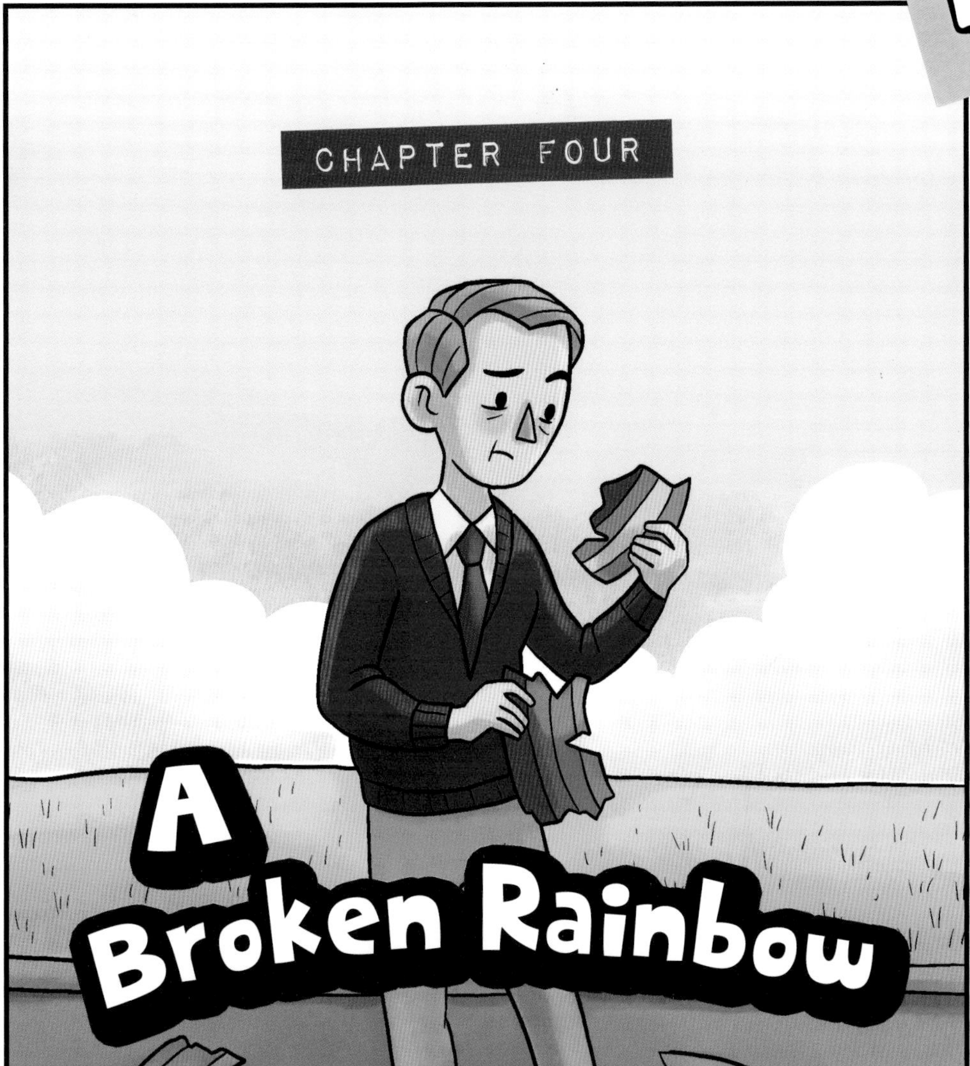
CHAPTER FOUR
A Broken Rainbow

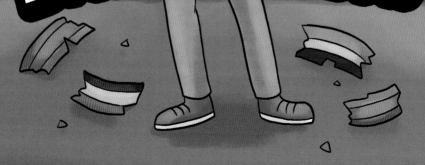

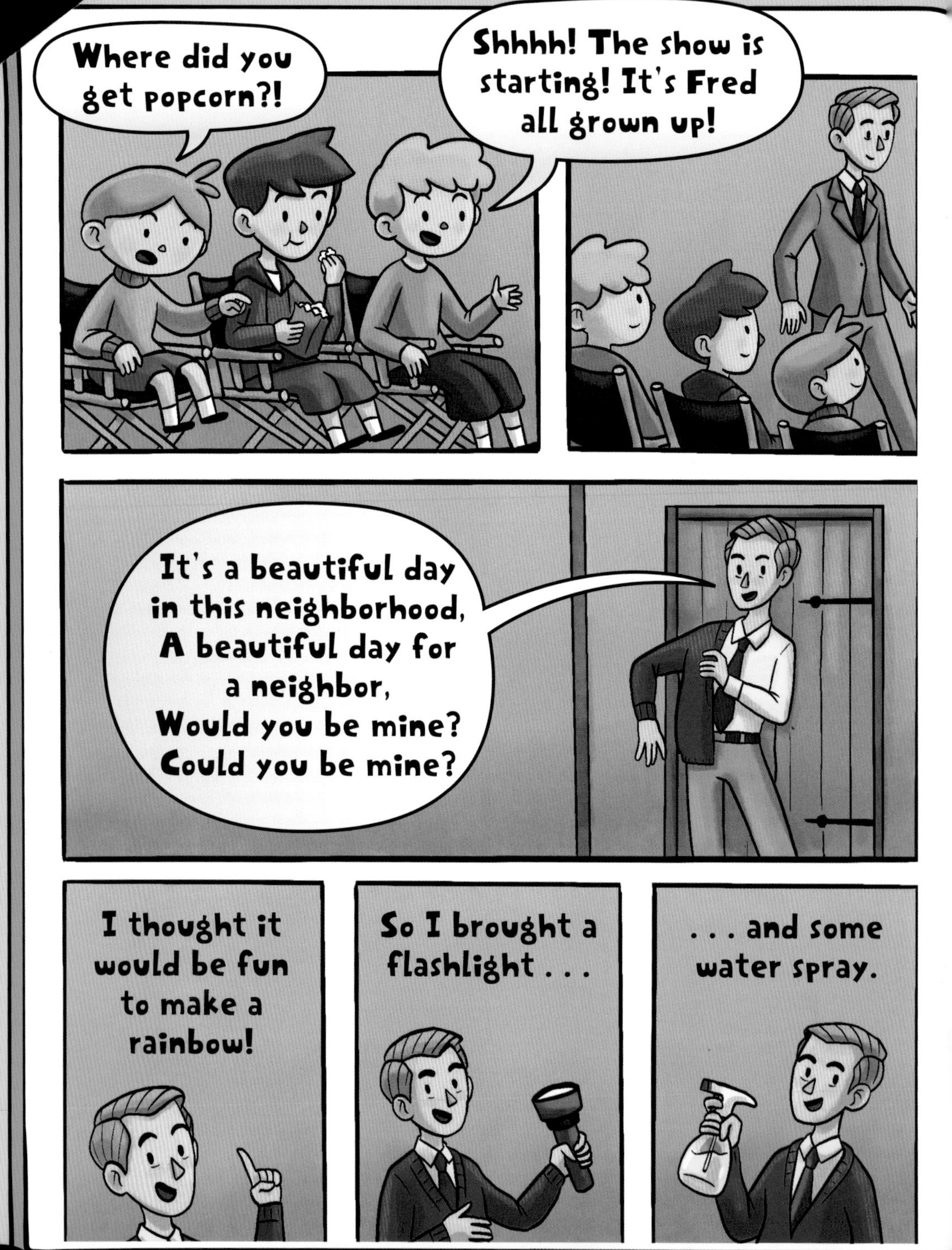
Where did you get popcorn?!
Shhhh! The show is starting! It's Fred all grown up!
It's a beautiful day in this neighborhood, A beautiful day for a neighbor, Would you be mine? Could you be mine?
I thought it would be fun to make a rainbow!
So I brought a flashlight . . .
. . . and some water spray.

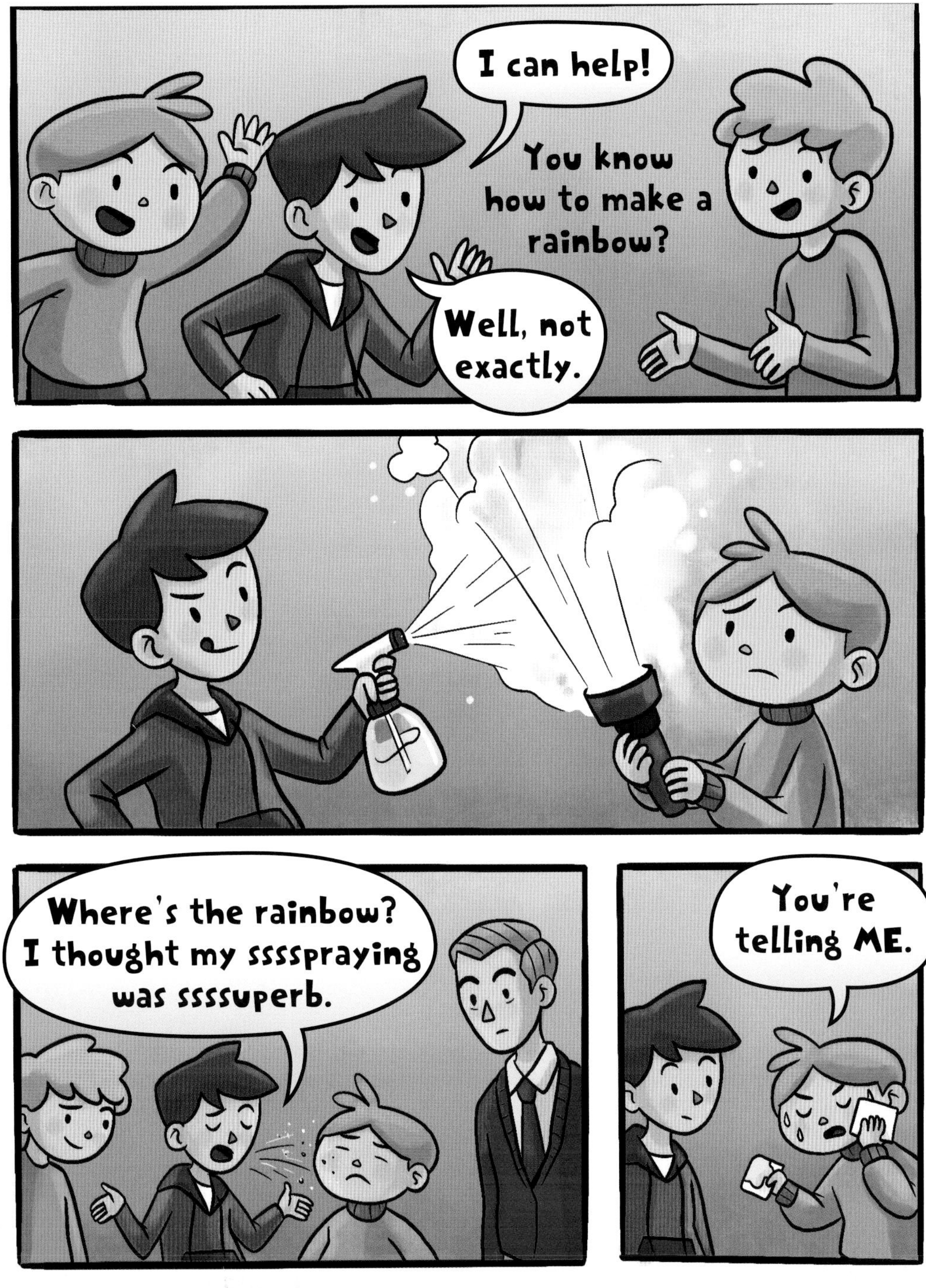
I can help!
You know how to make a rainbow?
Well, not exactly.
Where's the rainbow? I thought my sssspraying was sssssuperb.
You're telling ME.

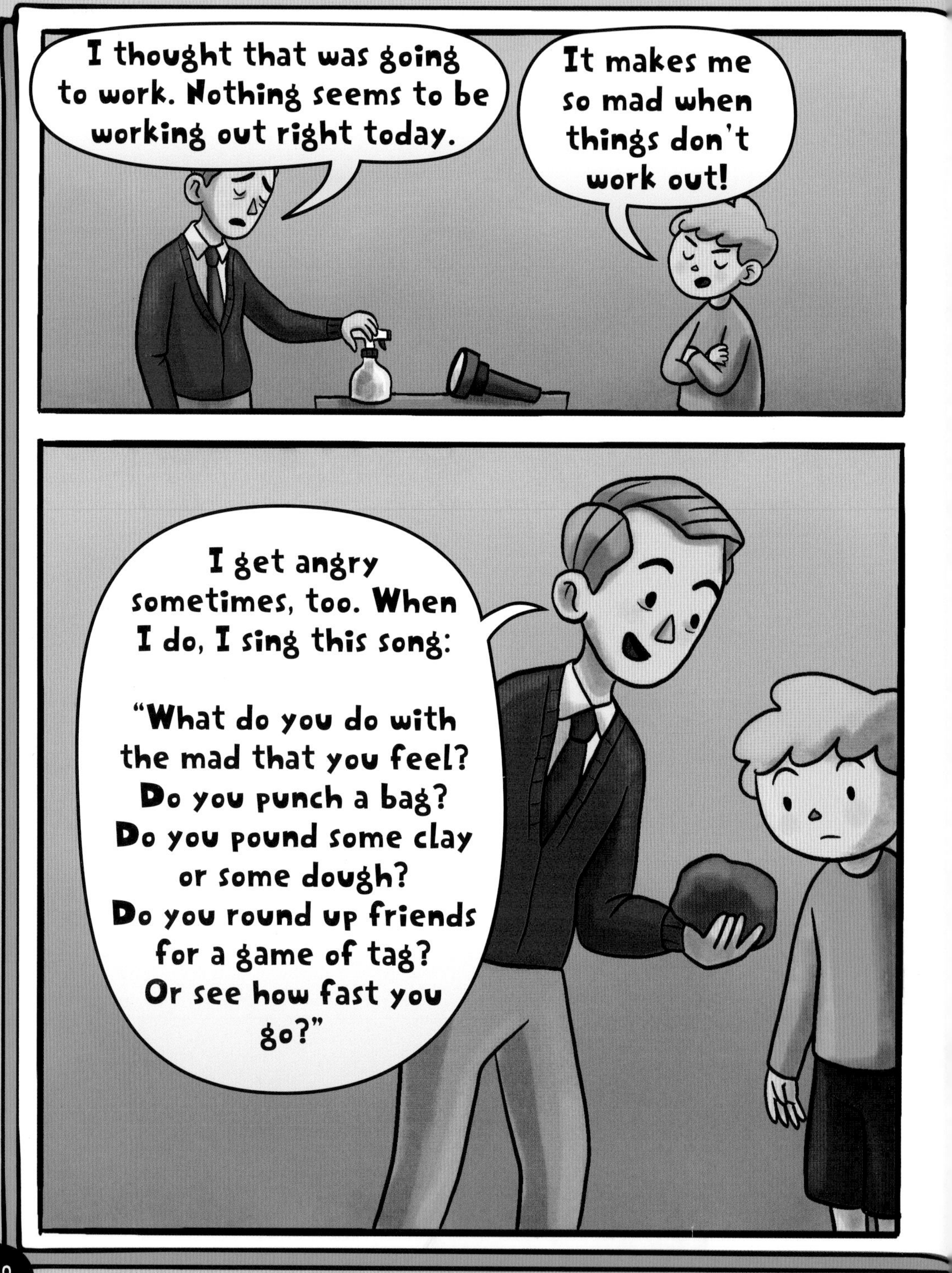
I thought that was going to work. Nothing seems to be working out right today.
It makes me so mad when things don't work out!
I get angry sometimes, too. When I do, I sing this song:
"What do you do with the mad that you feel? Do you punch a bag? Do you pound some clay or some dough? Do you round up friends for a game of tag? Or see how fast you go?"

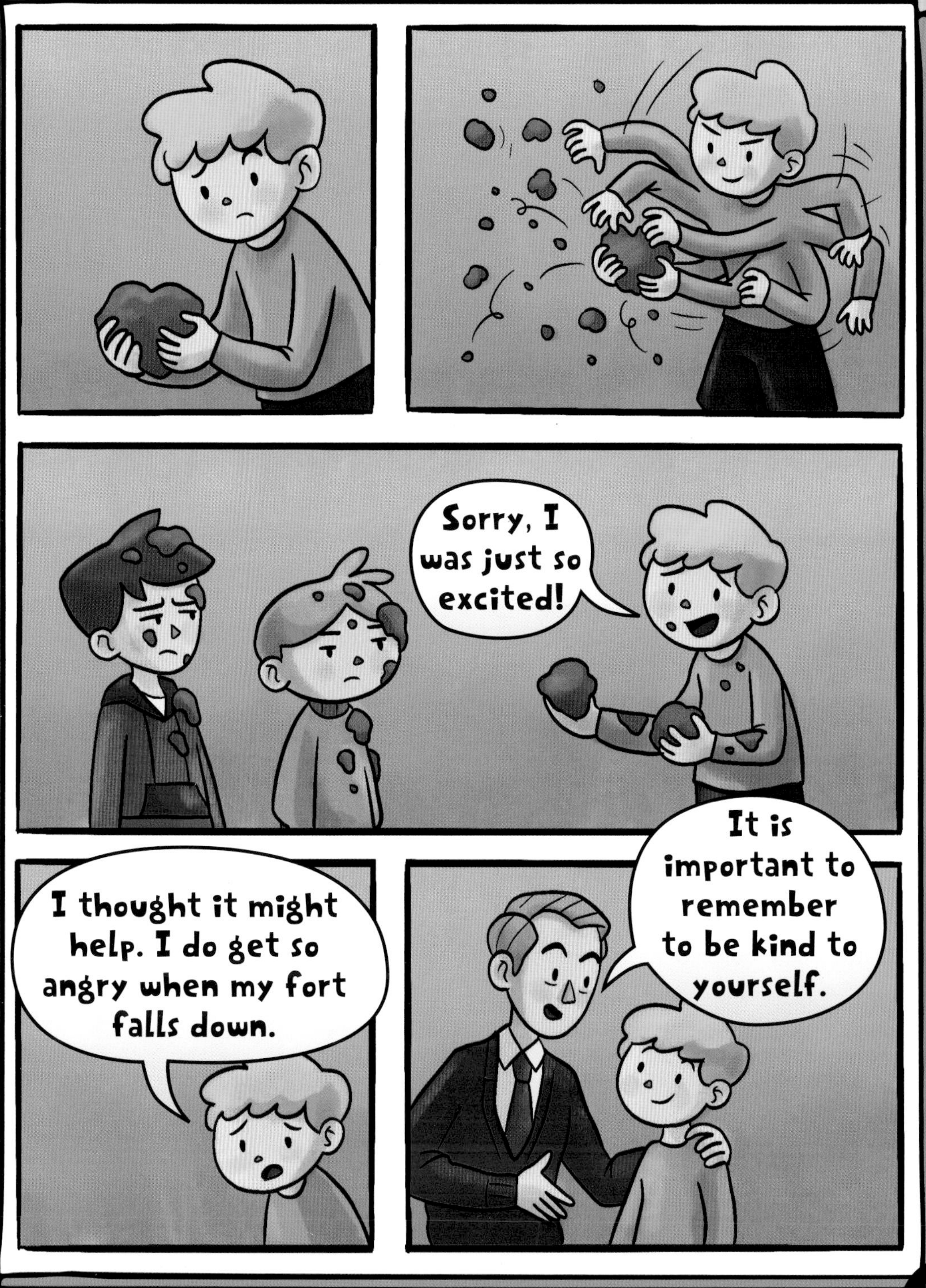
Sorry, I was just so excited!
I thought it might help. I do get so angry when my fort falls down.
It is important to remember to be kind to yourself.

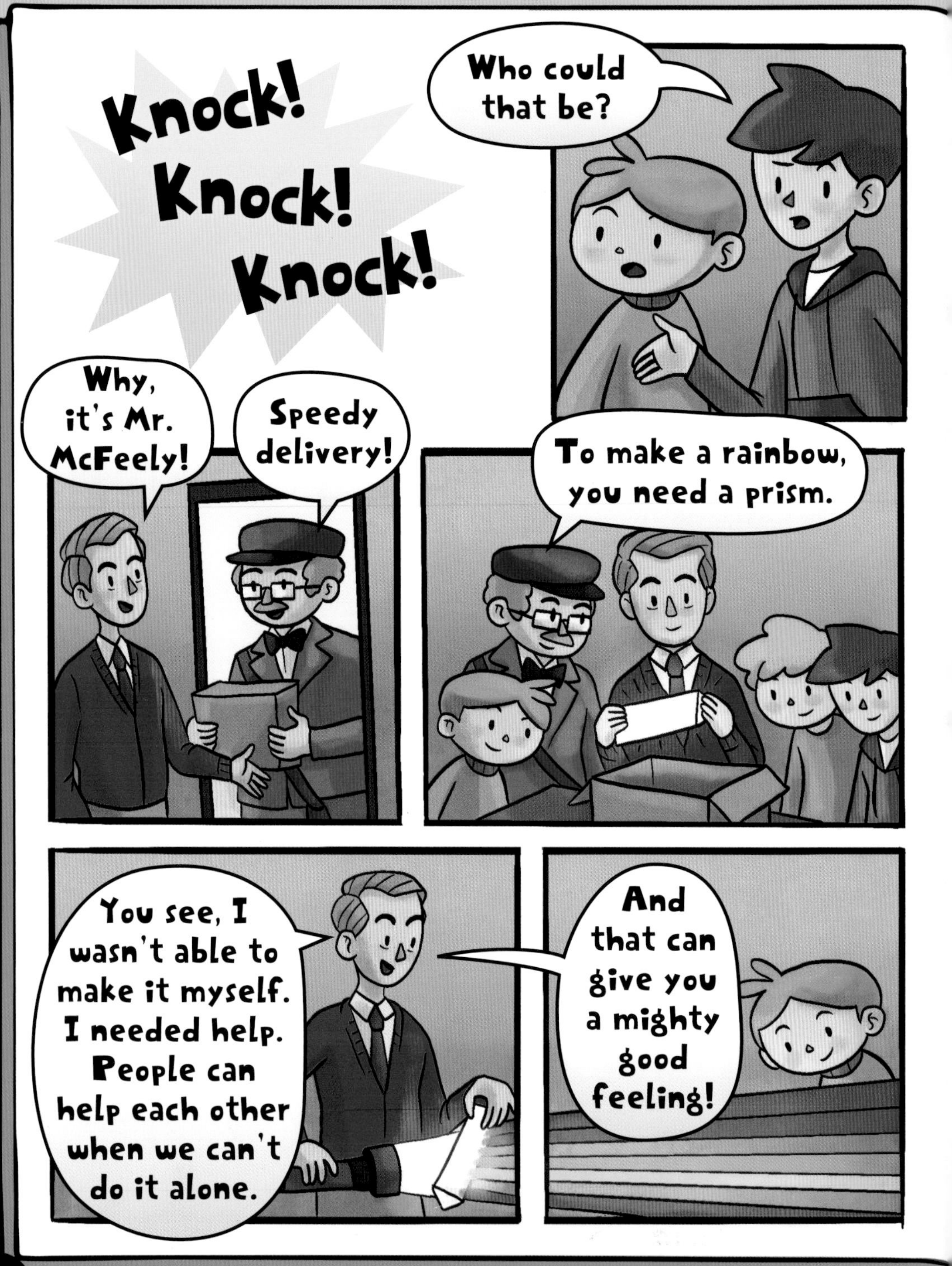
Knock!
Knock!
Knock!
Who could that be?
Why, it's Mr. McFeely!
Speedy delivery!
To make a rainbow, you need a prism.
You see, I wasn't able to make it myself. I needed help. People can help each other when we can't do it alone.
And that can give you a mighty good feeling!

CHAPTER FIVE

Mister Rogers Goes to Washington

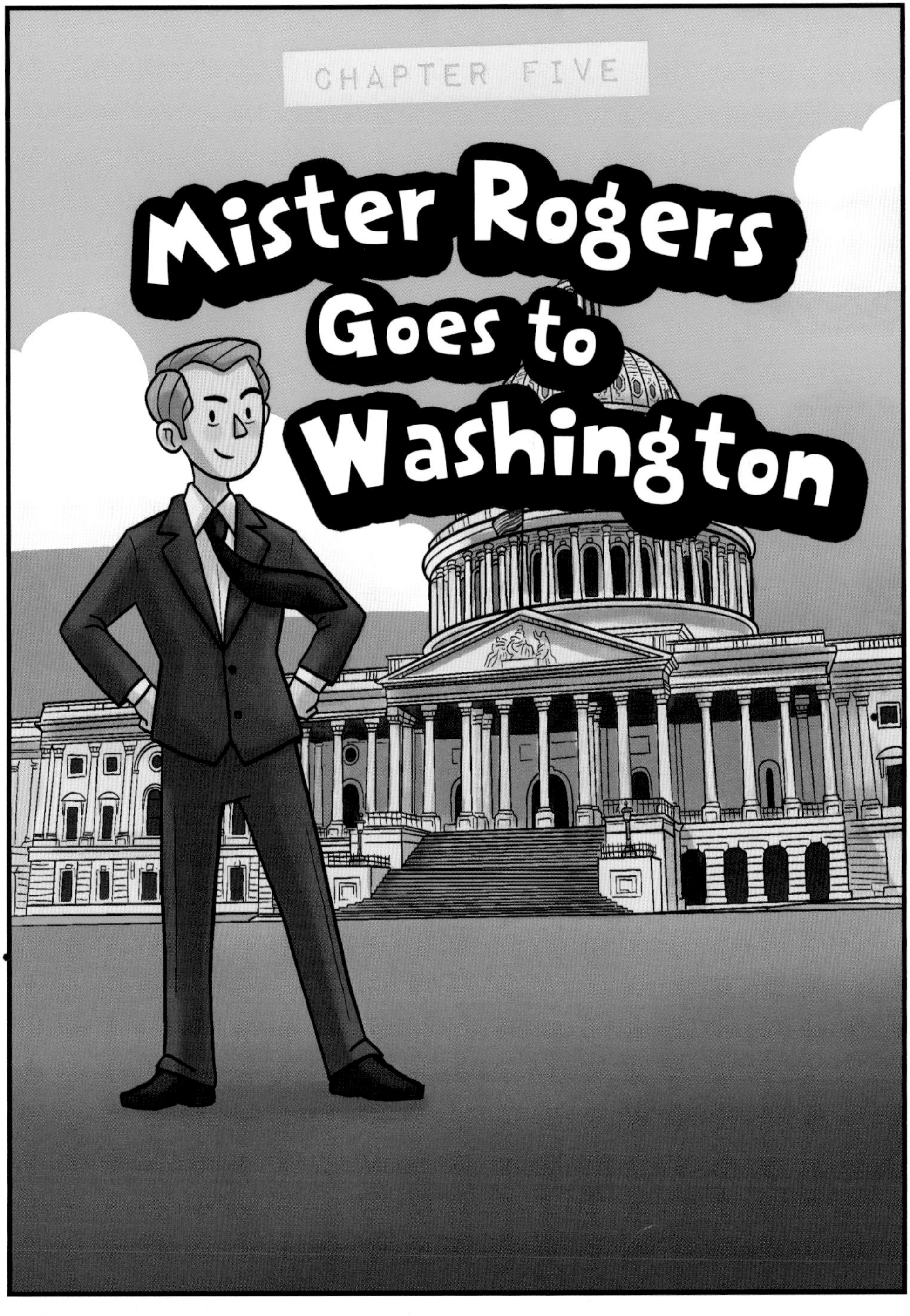

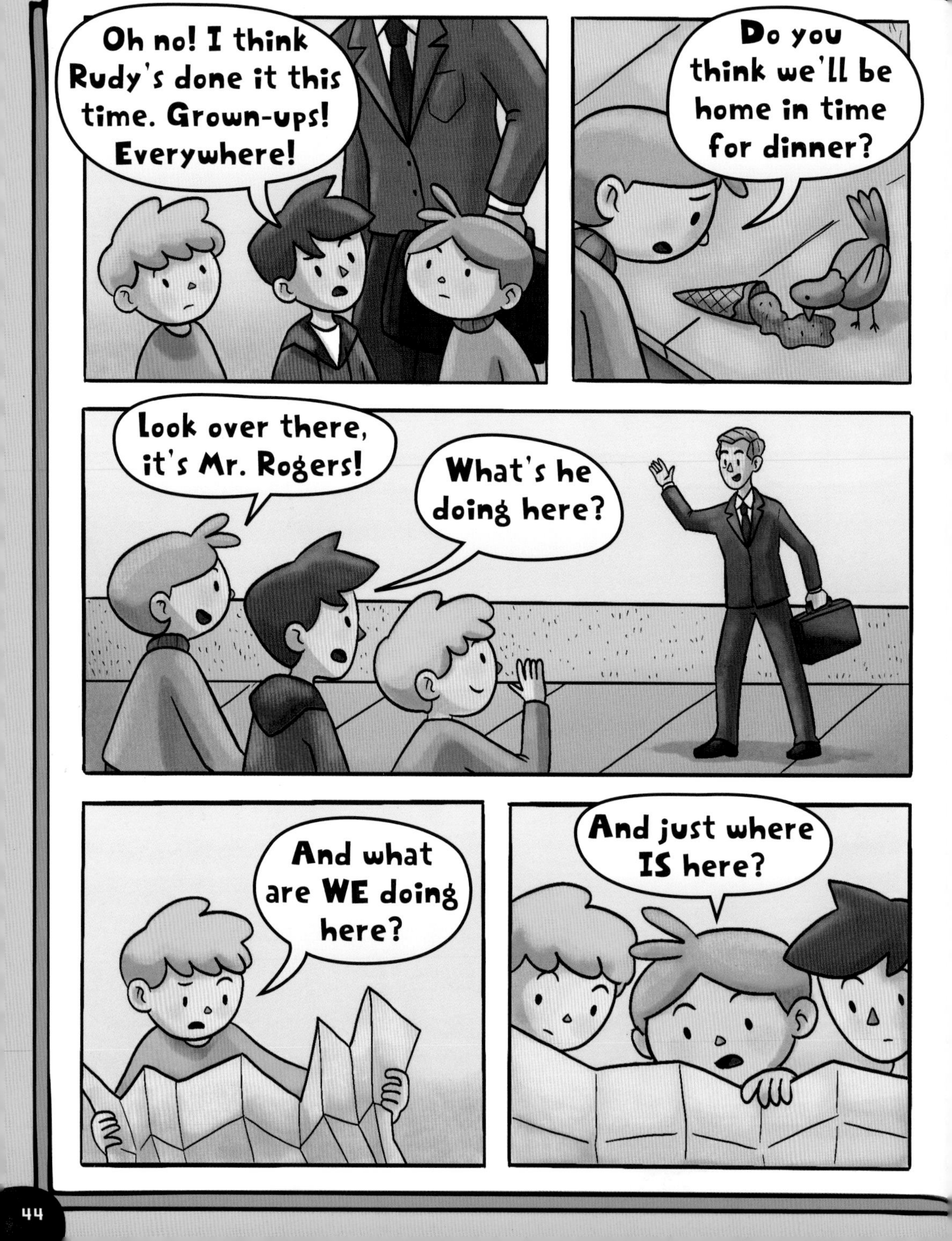
Oh no! I think Rudy's done it this time. Grown-ups! Everywhere!
Do you think we'll be home in time for dinner?
Look over there, it's Mr. Rogers!
What's he doing here?
And what are WE doing here?
And just where IS here?

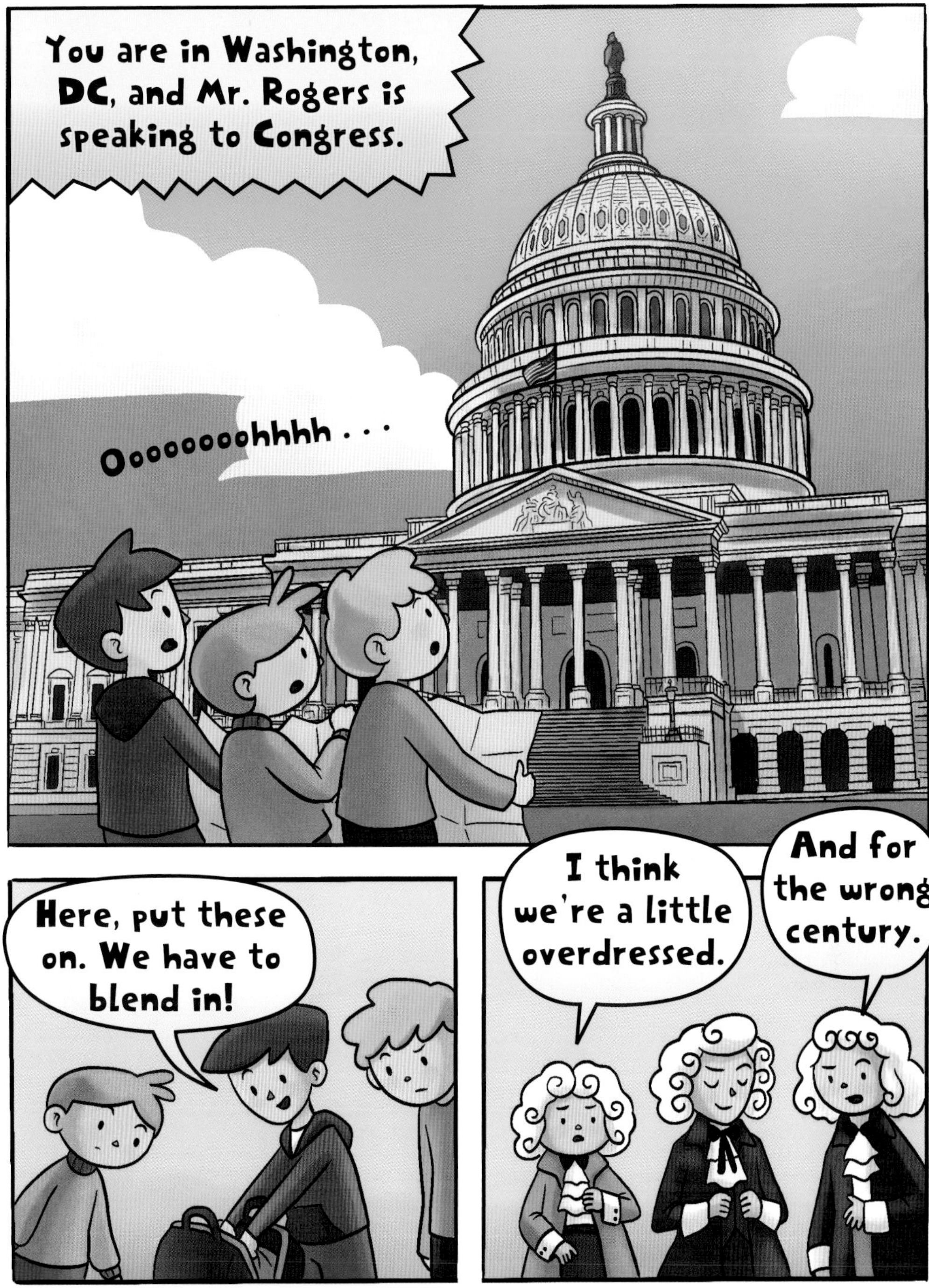

You are in Washington, DC, and Mr. Rogers is speaking to Congress.
Oooooooohhhh . . .
Here, put these on. We have to blend in!
I think we're a little overdressed.
And for the wrong century.

But I really look good with white hair!

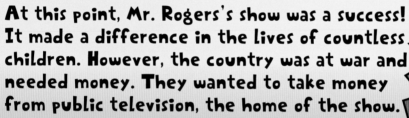

At this point, Mr. Rogers's show was a success! It made a difference in the lives of countless children. However, the country was at war and needed money. They wanted to take money from public television, the home of the show.

I hate it when I lose my allowance.

I usually save it for the ice cream truck.

Yes, well, Mr. Rogers was asking Congress for $20 million.

Ooh, that's a lot of ice cream!

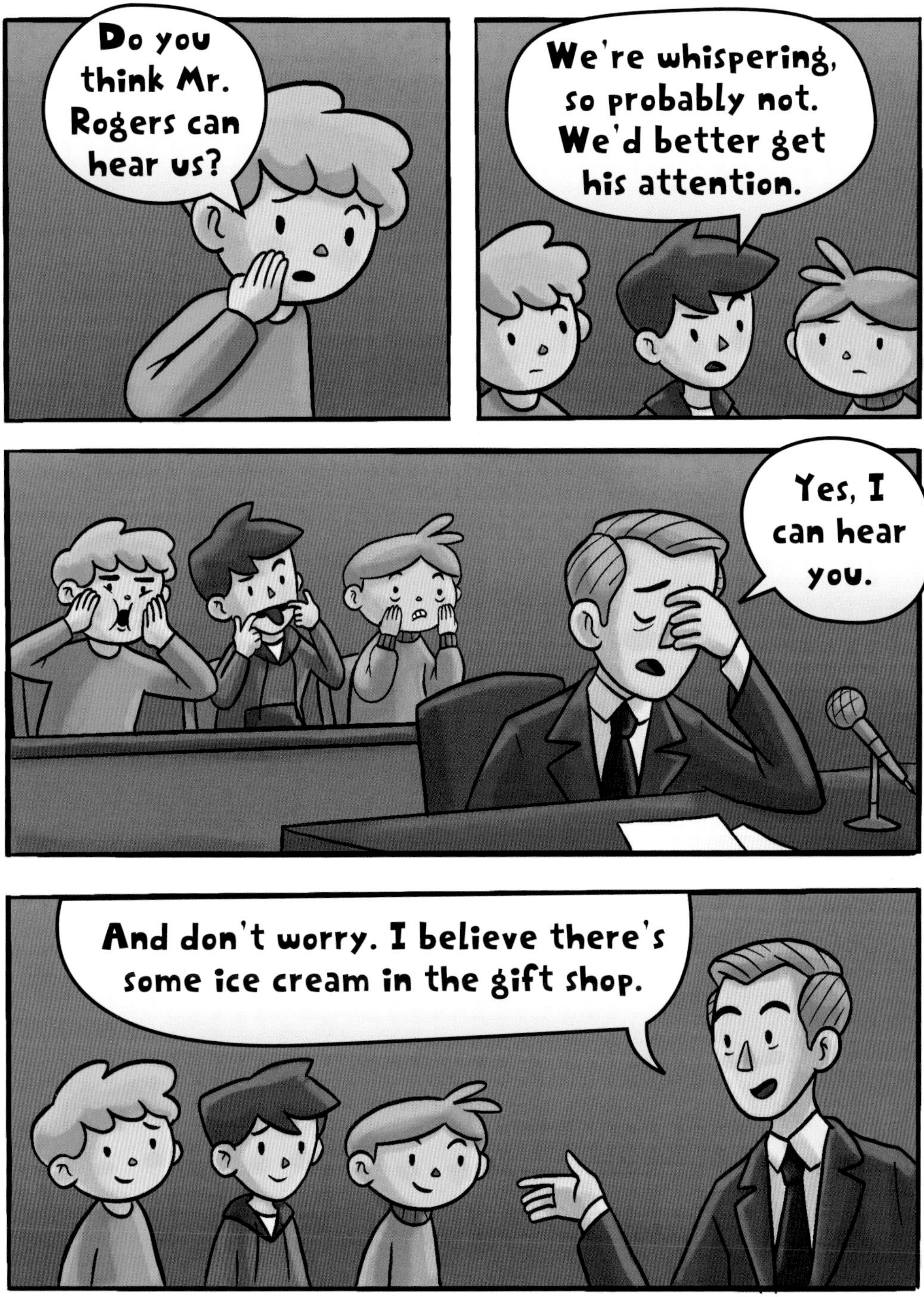
Do you think Mr. Rogers can hear us?
We're whispering, so probably not. We'd better get his attention.
Yes, I can hear you.
And don't worry. I believe there's some ice cream in the gift shop.

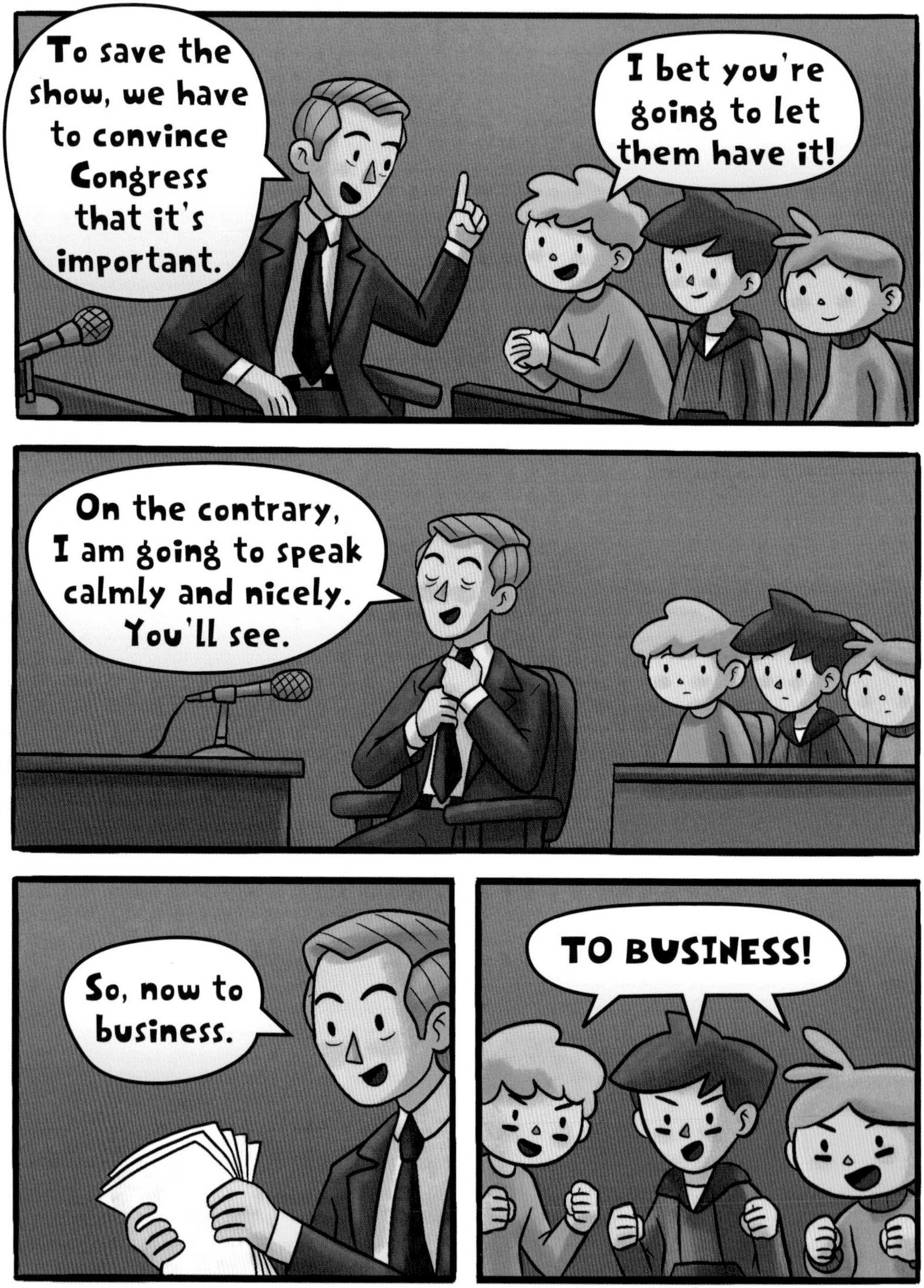
To save the show, we have to convince Congress that it's important.
I bet you're going to let them have it!
On the contrary, I am going to speak calmly and nicely. You'll see.
So, now to business.
TO BUSINESS!

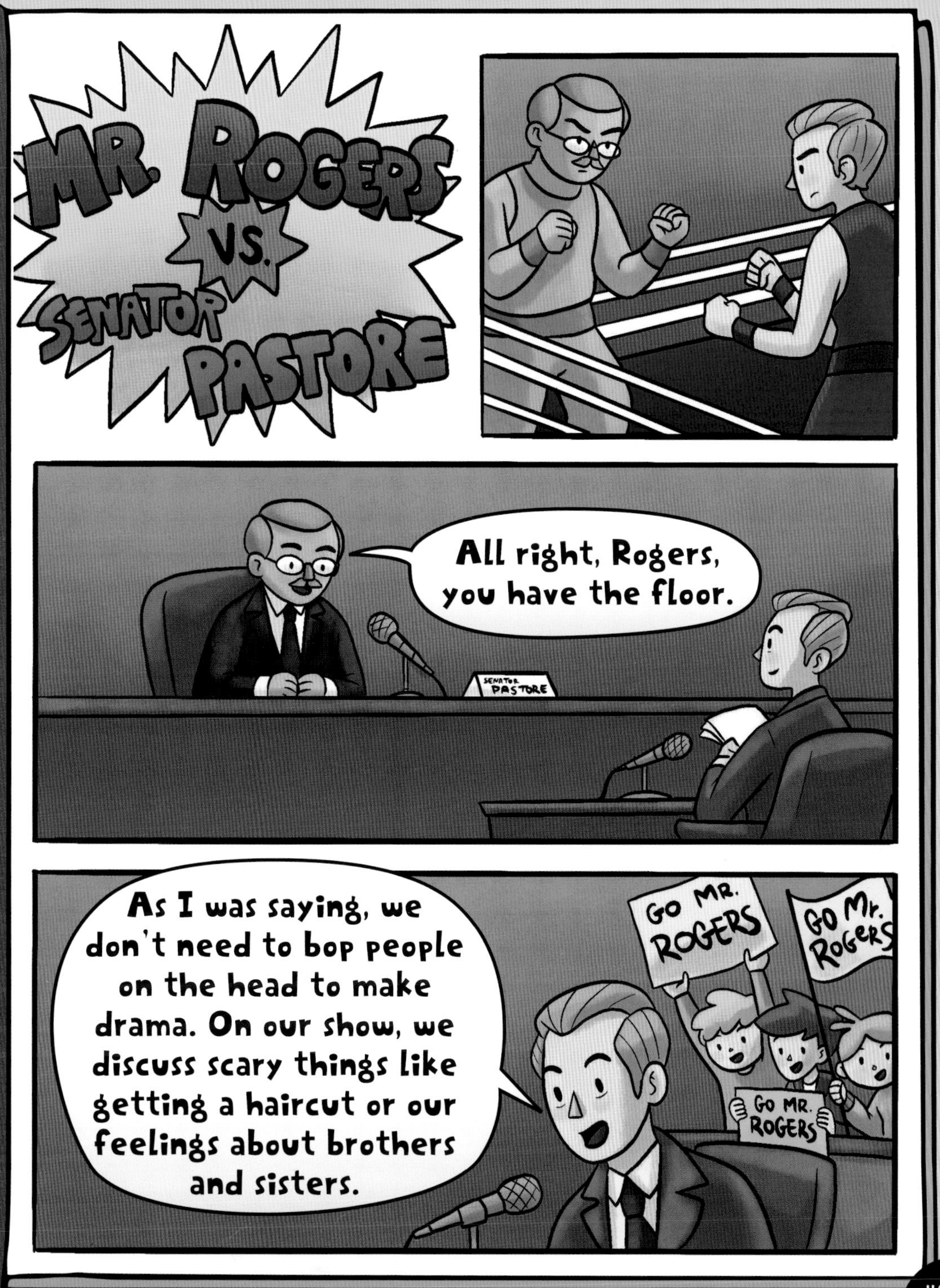
MR. ROGERS VS. SENATOR PASTORE
All right, Rogers, you have the floor.
SENATOR PASTORE
As I was saying, we don't need to bop people on the head to make drama. On our show, we discuss scary things like getting a haircut or our feelings about brothers and sisters.
GO MR. ROGERS
GO Mr. ROGERS
GO MR. ROGERS

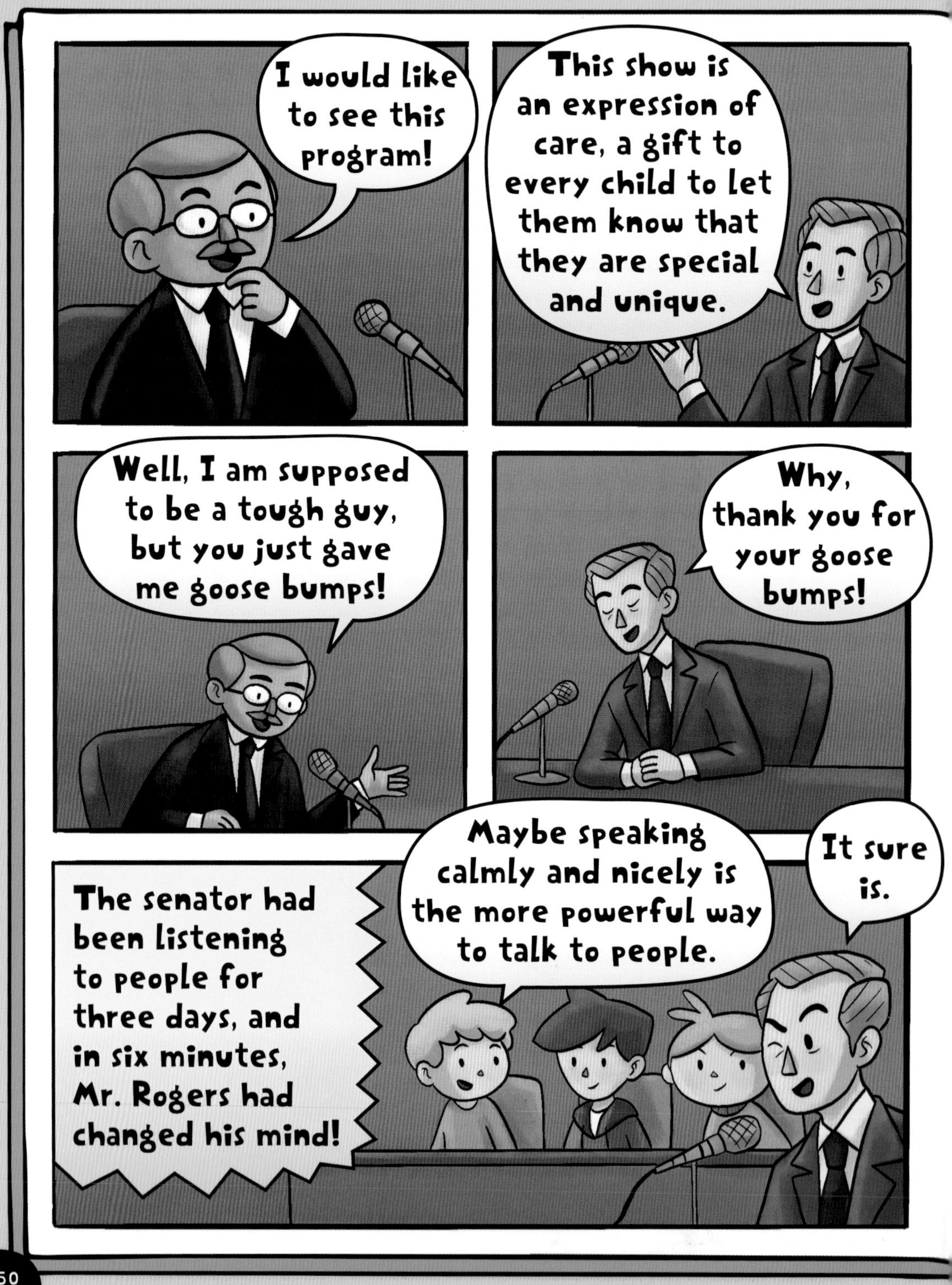
I would like to see this program!
This show is an expression of care, a gift to every child to let them know that they are special and unique.
Well, I am supposed to be a tough guy, but you just gave me goose bumps!
Why, thank you for your goose bumps!
The senator had been listening to people for three days, and in six minutes, Mr. Rogers had changed his mind!
Maybe speaking calmly and nicely is the more powerful way to talk to people.
It sure is.

CHAPTER SIX

The Pool with More Than Enough Room

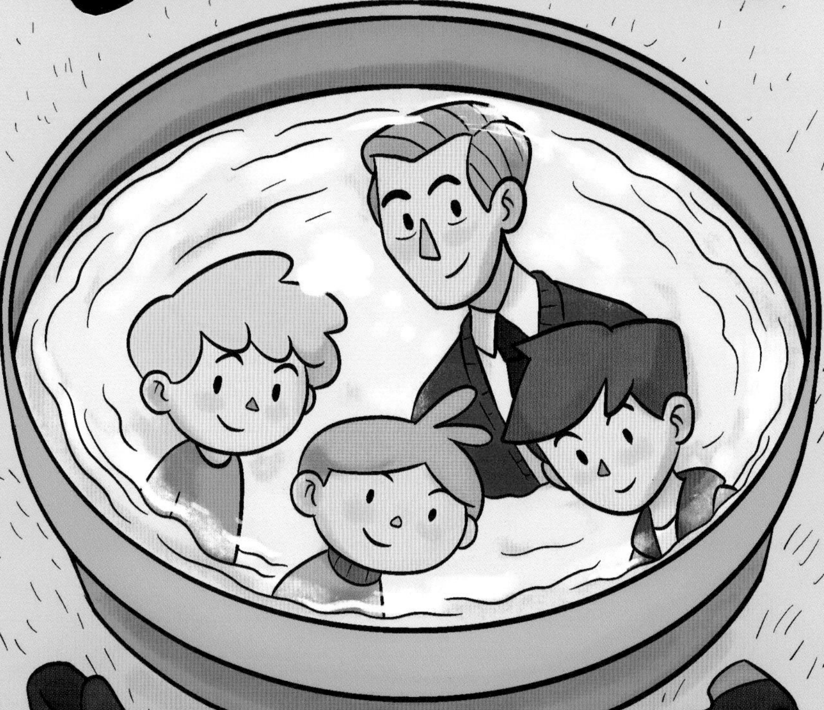

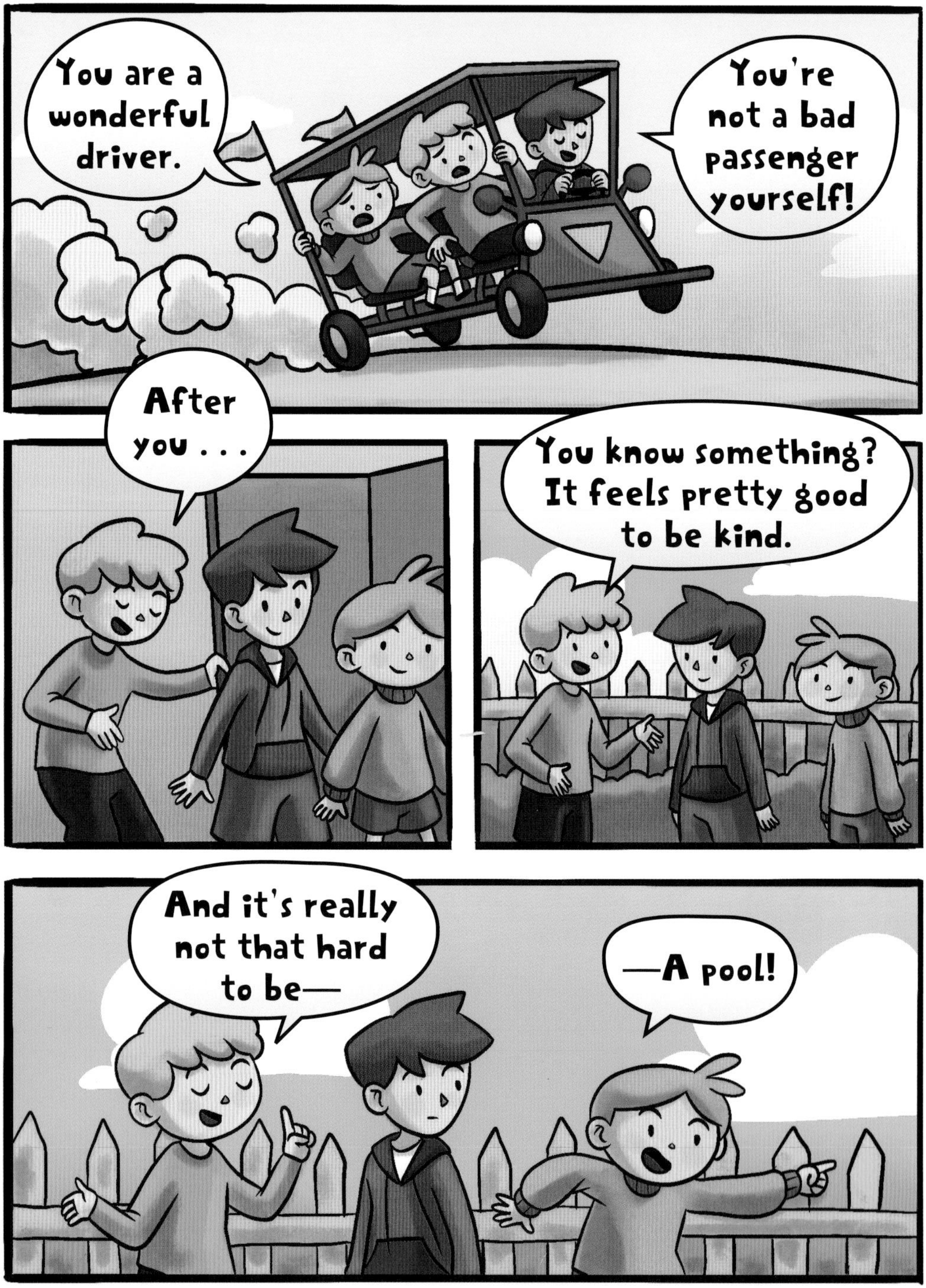
You are a wonderful driver.
You're not a bad passenger yourself!
After you . . .
You know something? It feels pretty good to be kind.
And it's really not that hard to be—
—A pool!

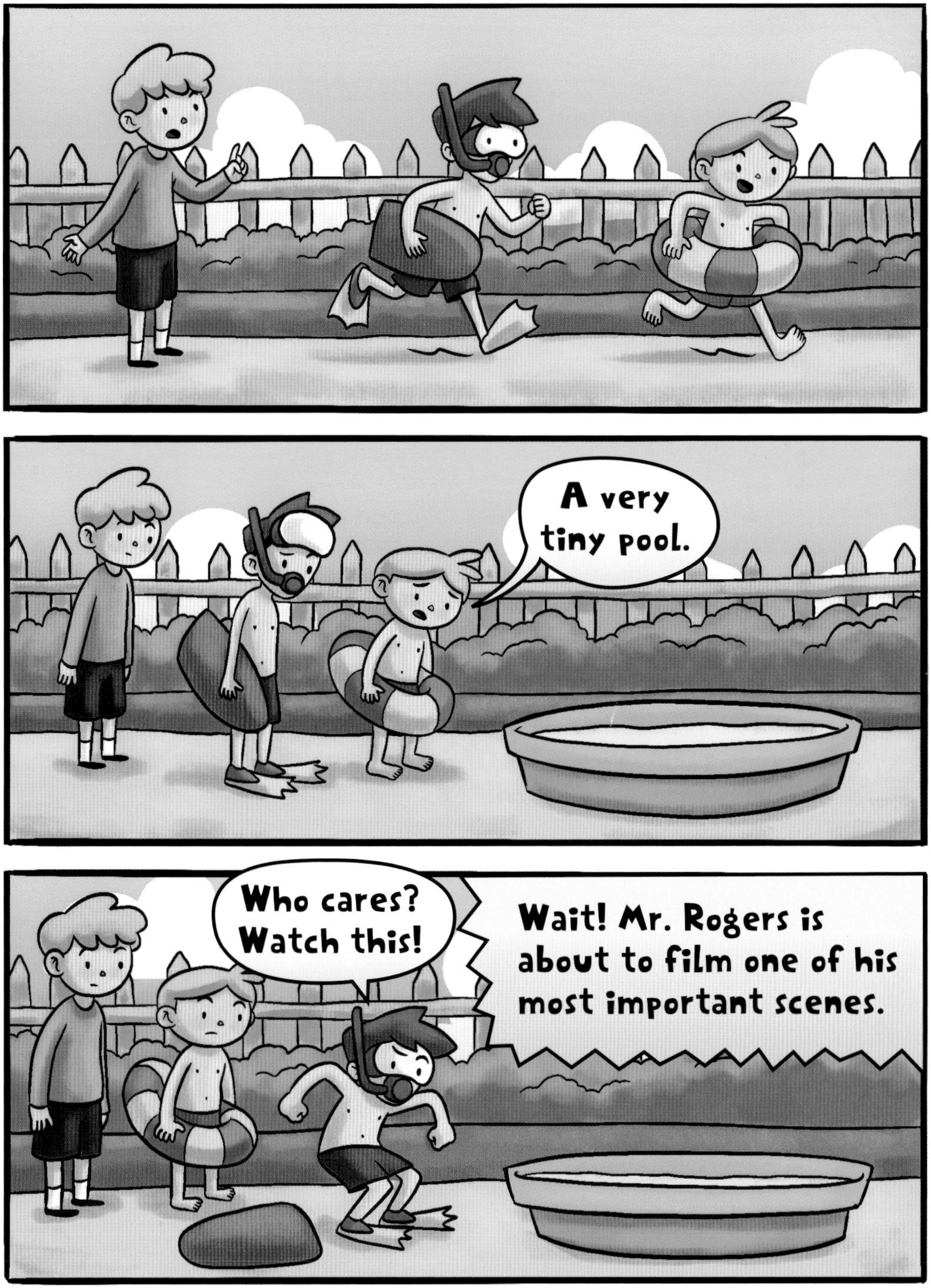
A very tiny pool.
Who cares? Watch this!
Wait! Mr. Rogers is about to film one of his most important scenes.

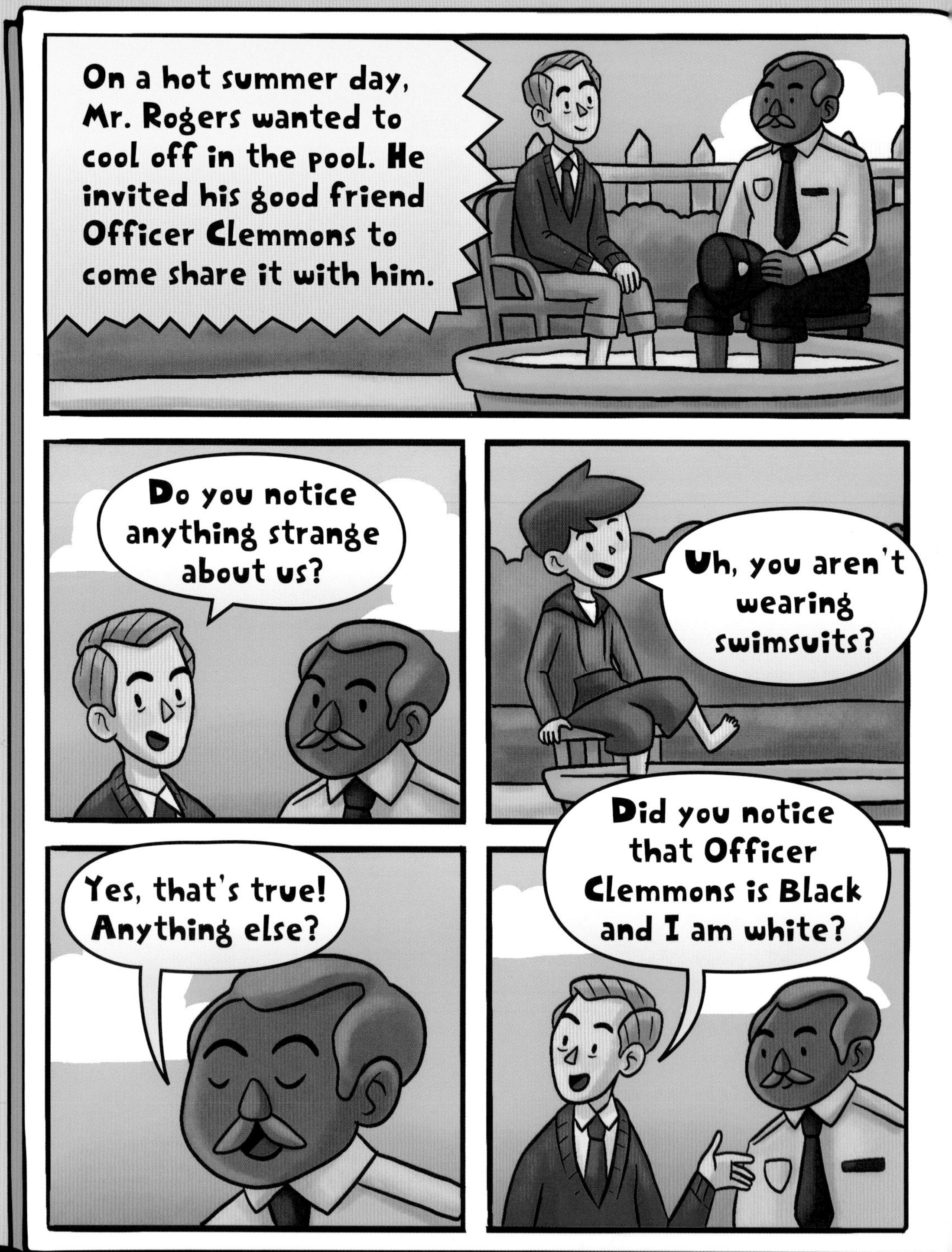
On a hot summer day, Mr. Rogers wanted to cool off in the pool. He invited his good friend Officer Clemmons to come share it with him.
Do you notice anything strange about us?
Uh, you aren't wearing swimsuits?
Yes, that's true! Anything else?
Did you notice that Officer Clemmons is Black and I am white?

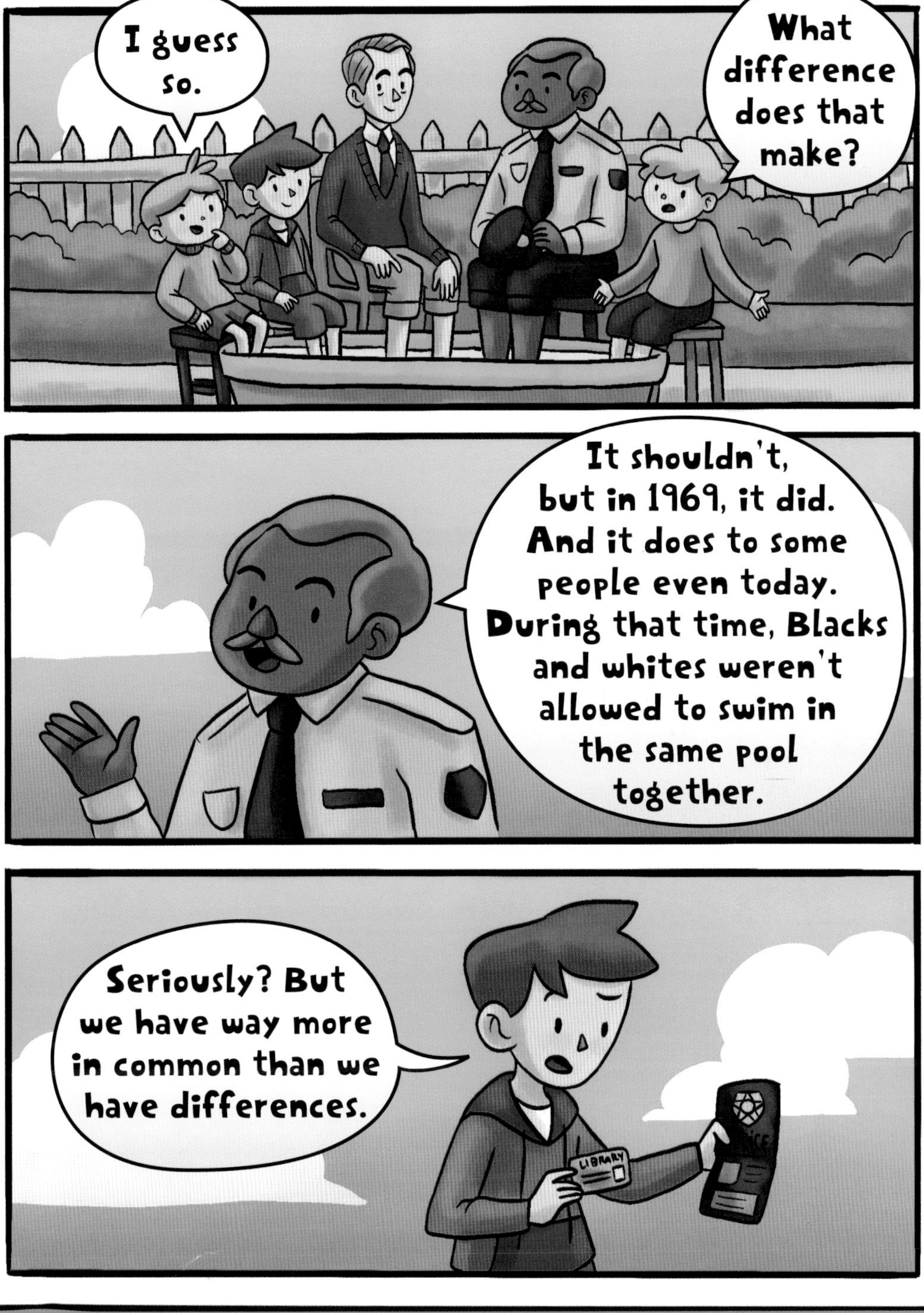
I guess so.
What difference does that make?
It shouldn't, but in 1969, it did. And it does to some people even today. During that time, Blacks and whites weren't allowed to swim in the same pool together.
Seriously? But we have way more in common than we have differences.
LIBRARY

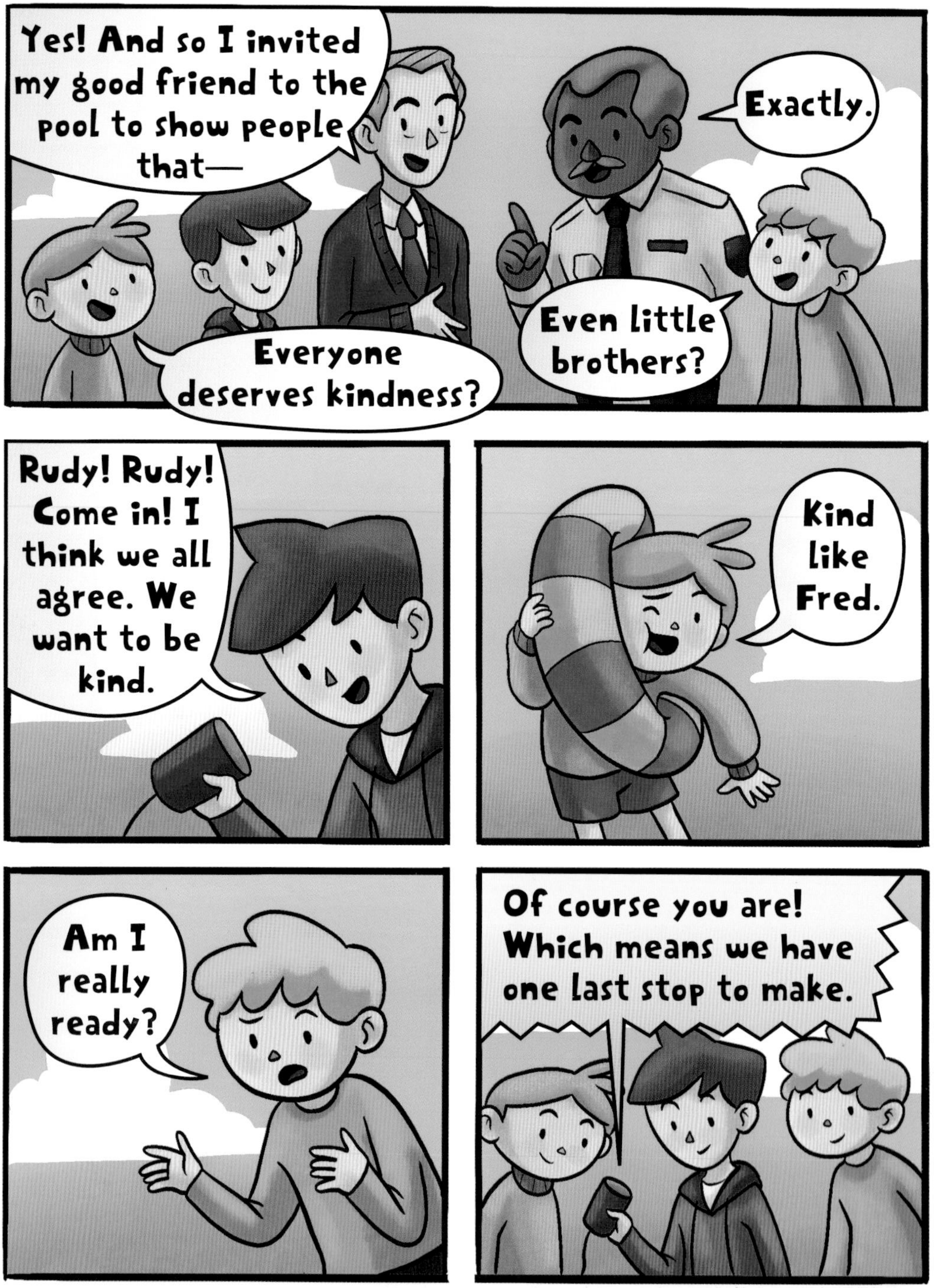
Yes! And so I invited my good friend to the pool to show people that—
Exactly.
Everyone deserves kindness?
Even little brothers?
Rudy! Rudy! Come in! I think we all agree. We want to be kind.
Kind like Fred.
Am I really ready?
Of course you are! Which means we have one last stop to make.

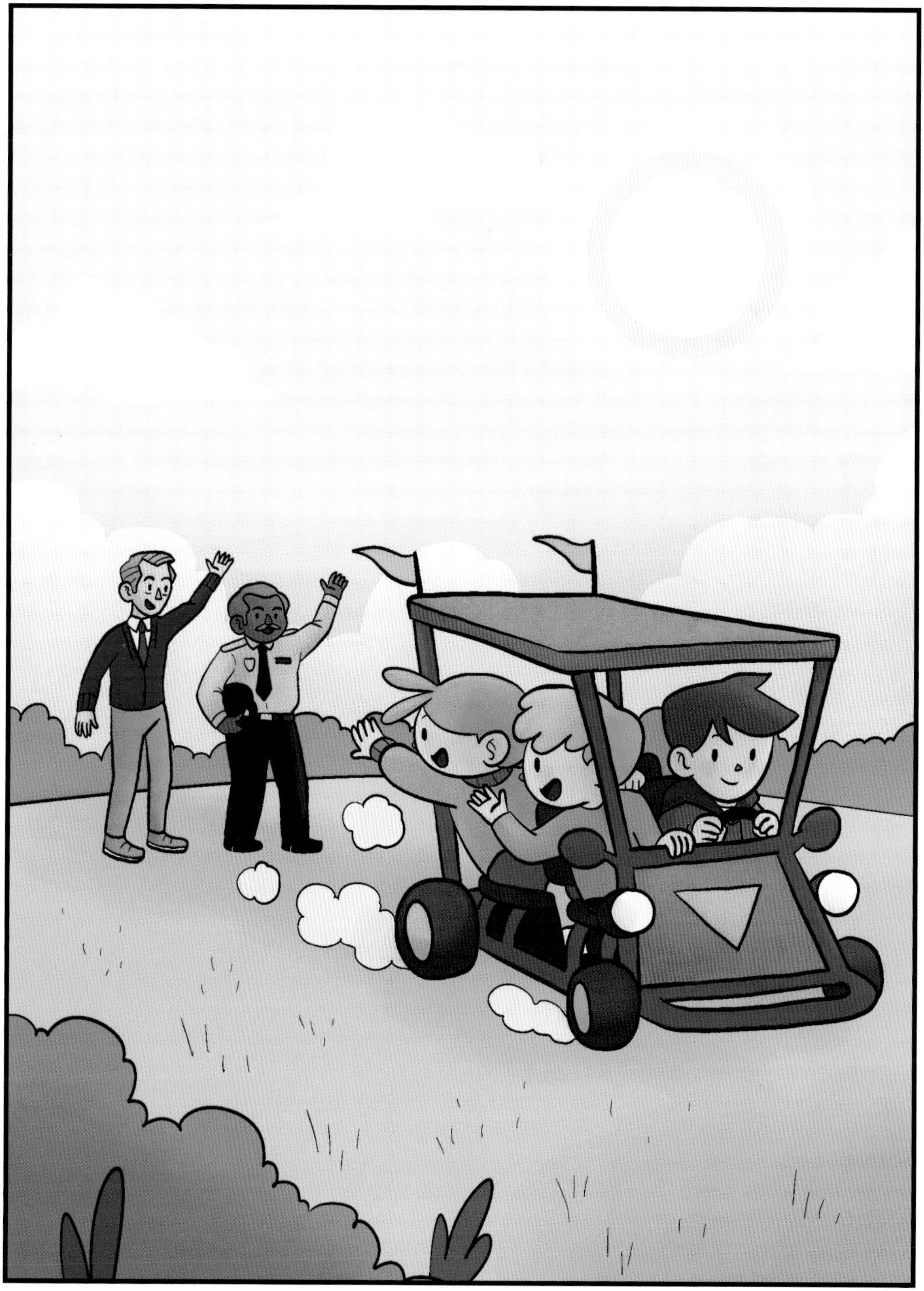

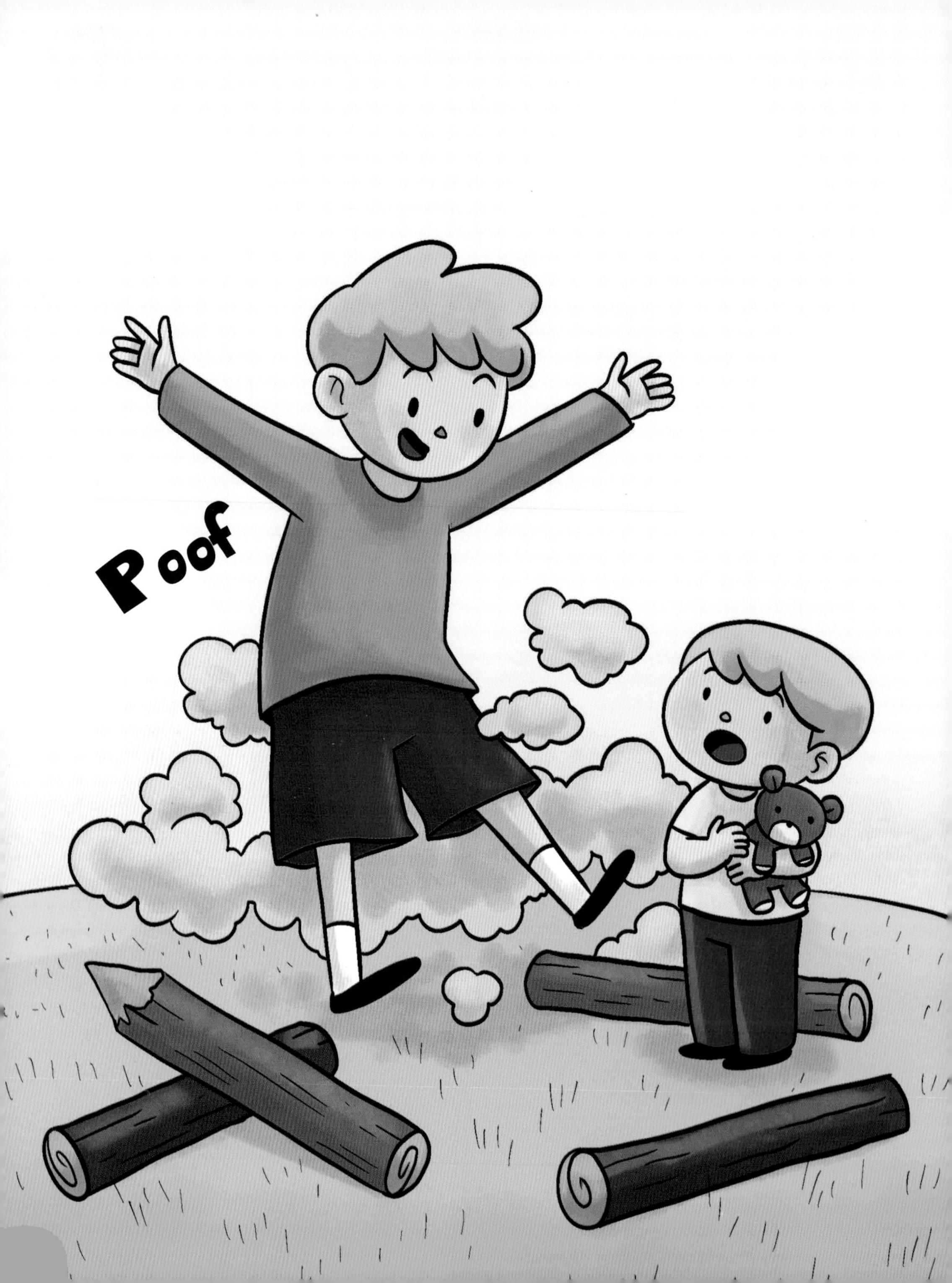
Poof

CHAPTER SEVEN

Hello, Neighbor

"Hello, neighbor!" Charlie popped up from nowhere like a jack-in-the-box. "I was wondering where you were."

"I was inside," said Teddy, who hung his head. "I thought you wanted me to be far away."

"That's what I thought, but then I realized something."

Teddy perked up. "What's that?"

"I have built this fort three times," Charlie admitted, "and it has fallen down each time."

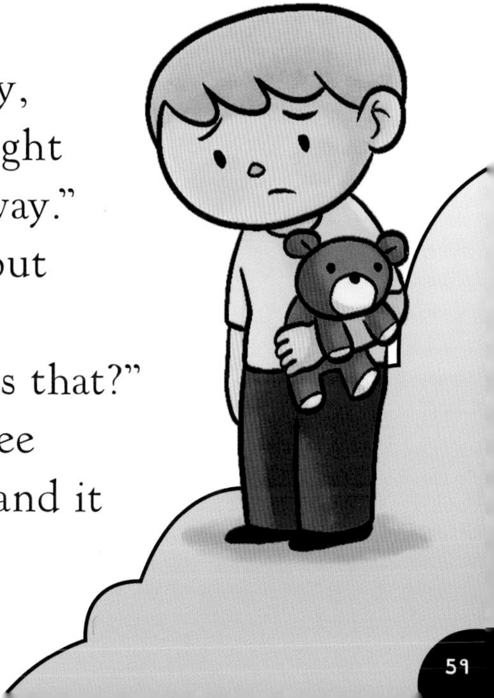

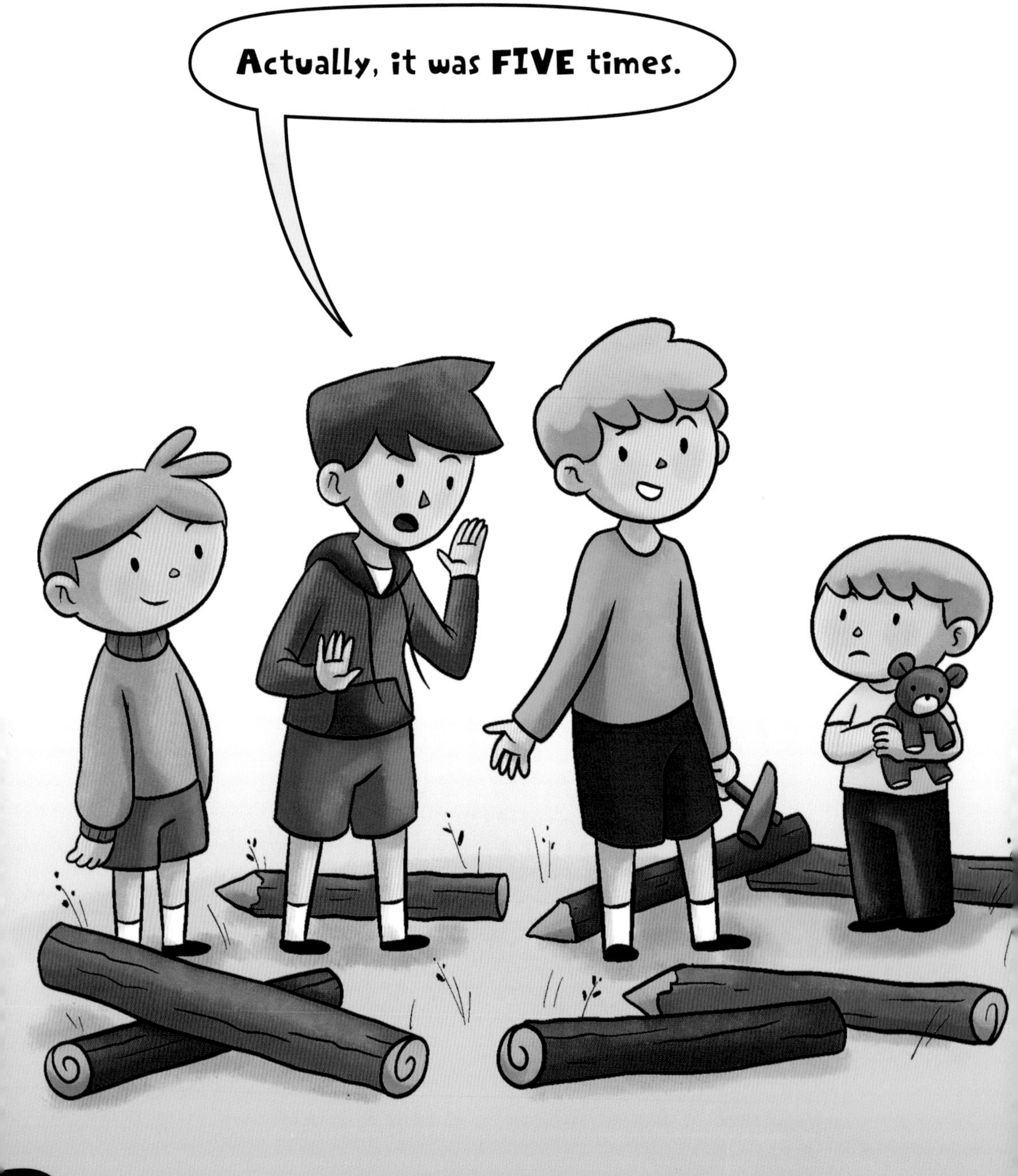
Actually, it was **FIVE** times.

"Thank you, Lucky." Charlie sighed. "The point is, maybe if we build this one together, it'll stay up."

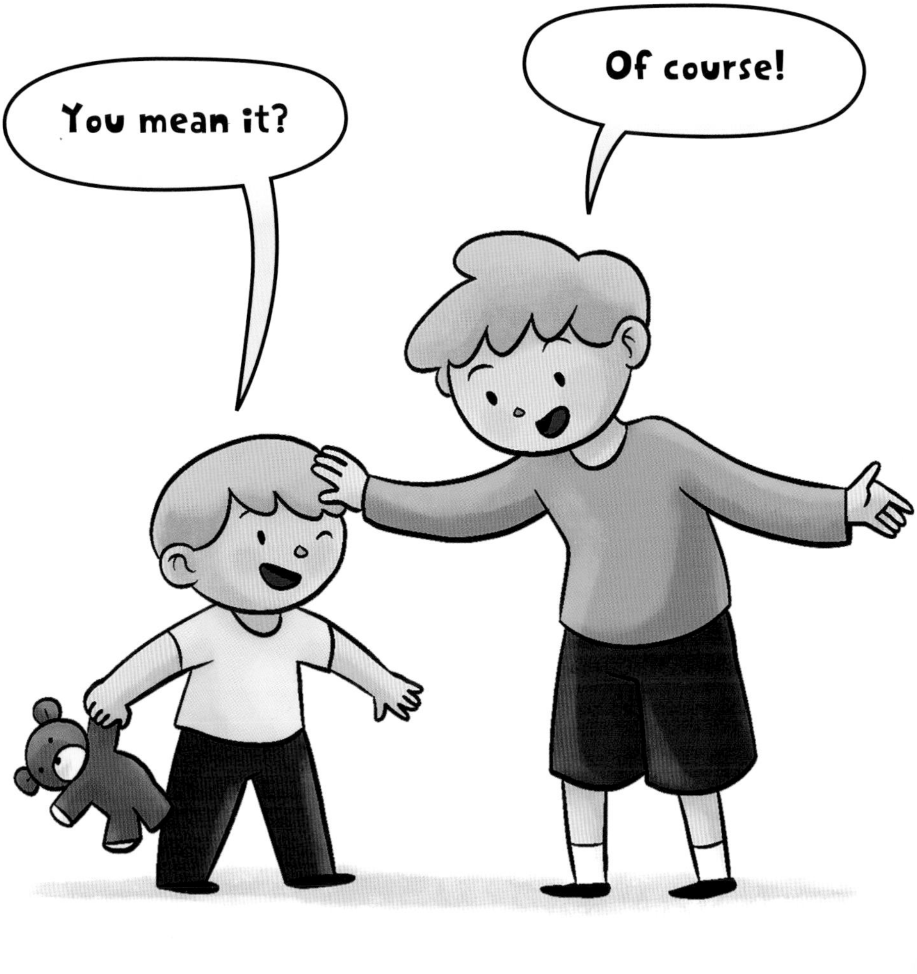
You mean it?
Of course!

Then, with the world's biggest smile, Teddy did something that hadn't happened in a long time.

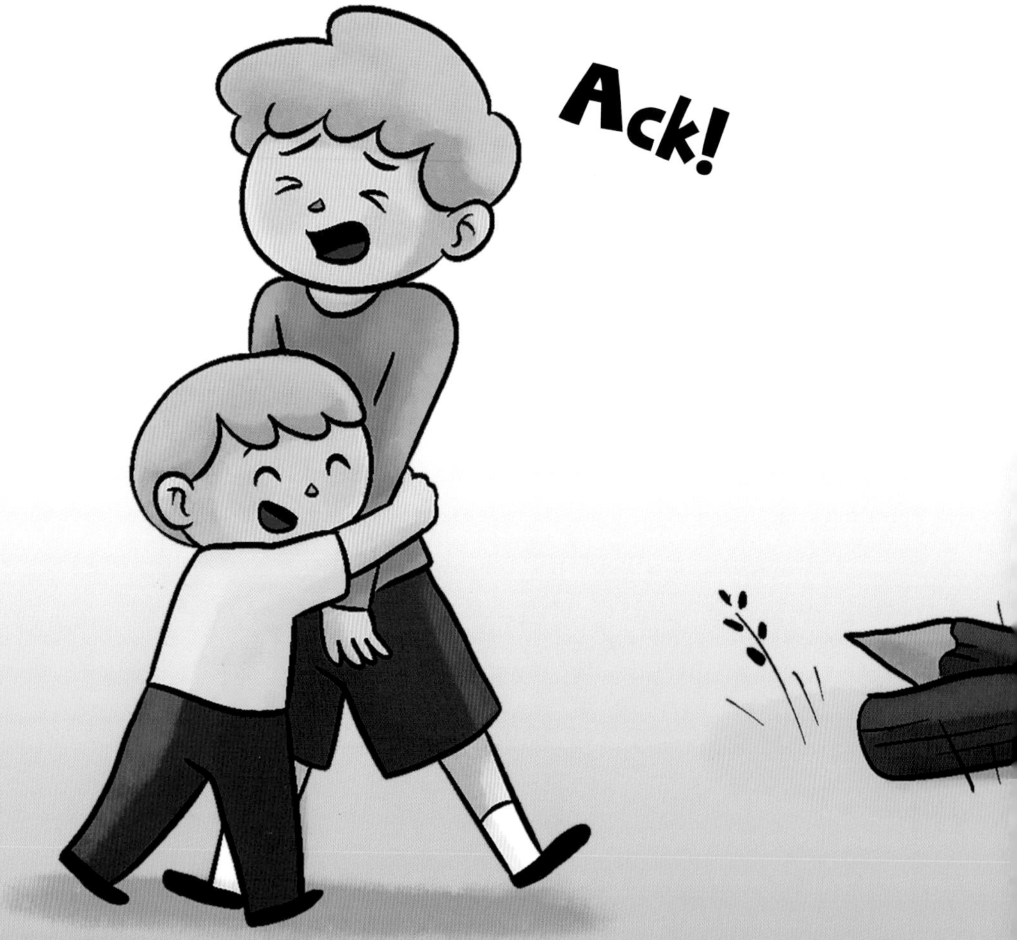
Ack!

Lucky jumped up onto the construction site and put his hands on his hips.

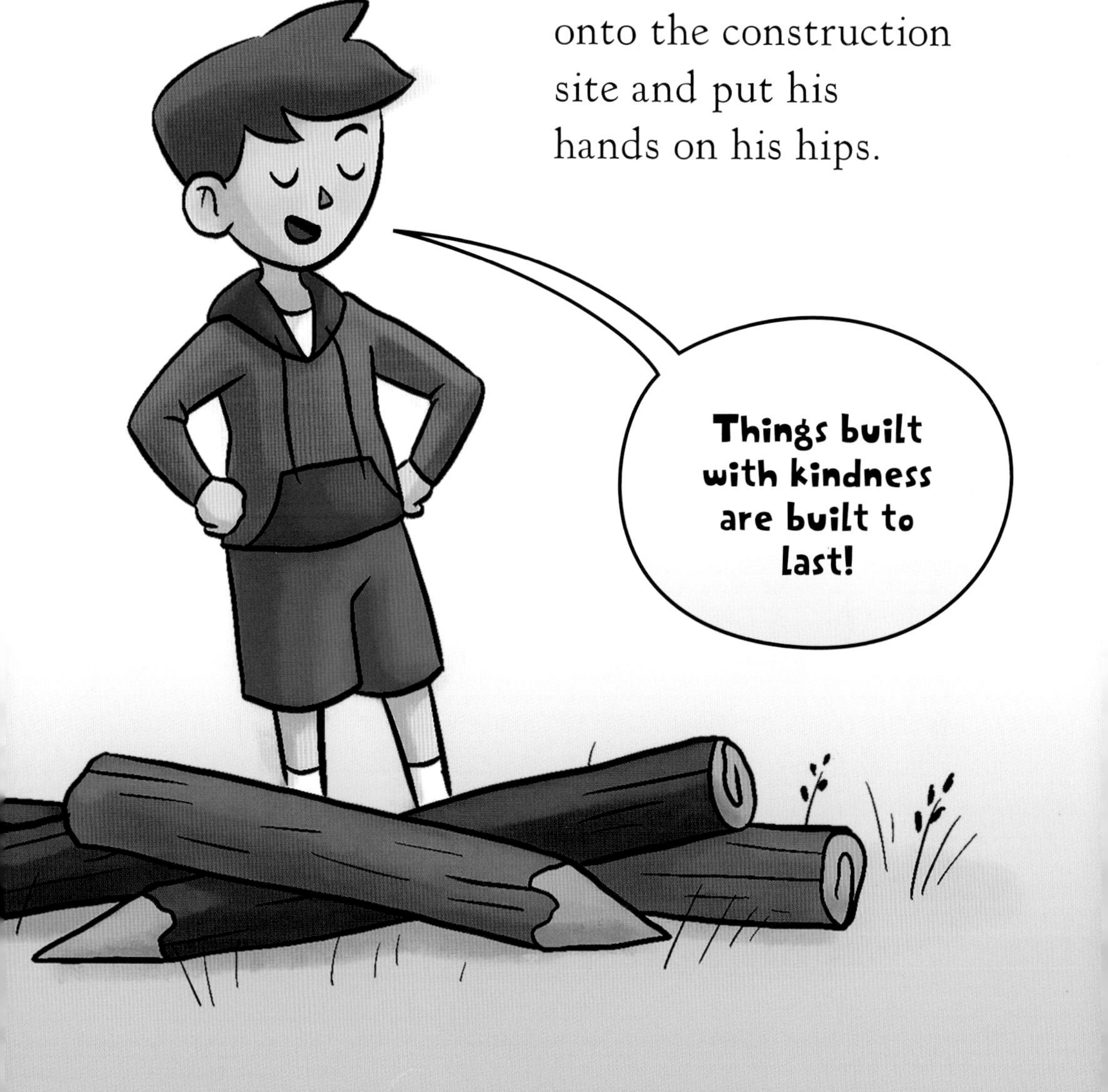
Things built with kindness are built to last!

"Thank goodness for Mr. Rogers! We couldn't have done this without him," said Charlie.

Lucky cleared his throat, and Red whispered something in Charlie's ear.

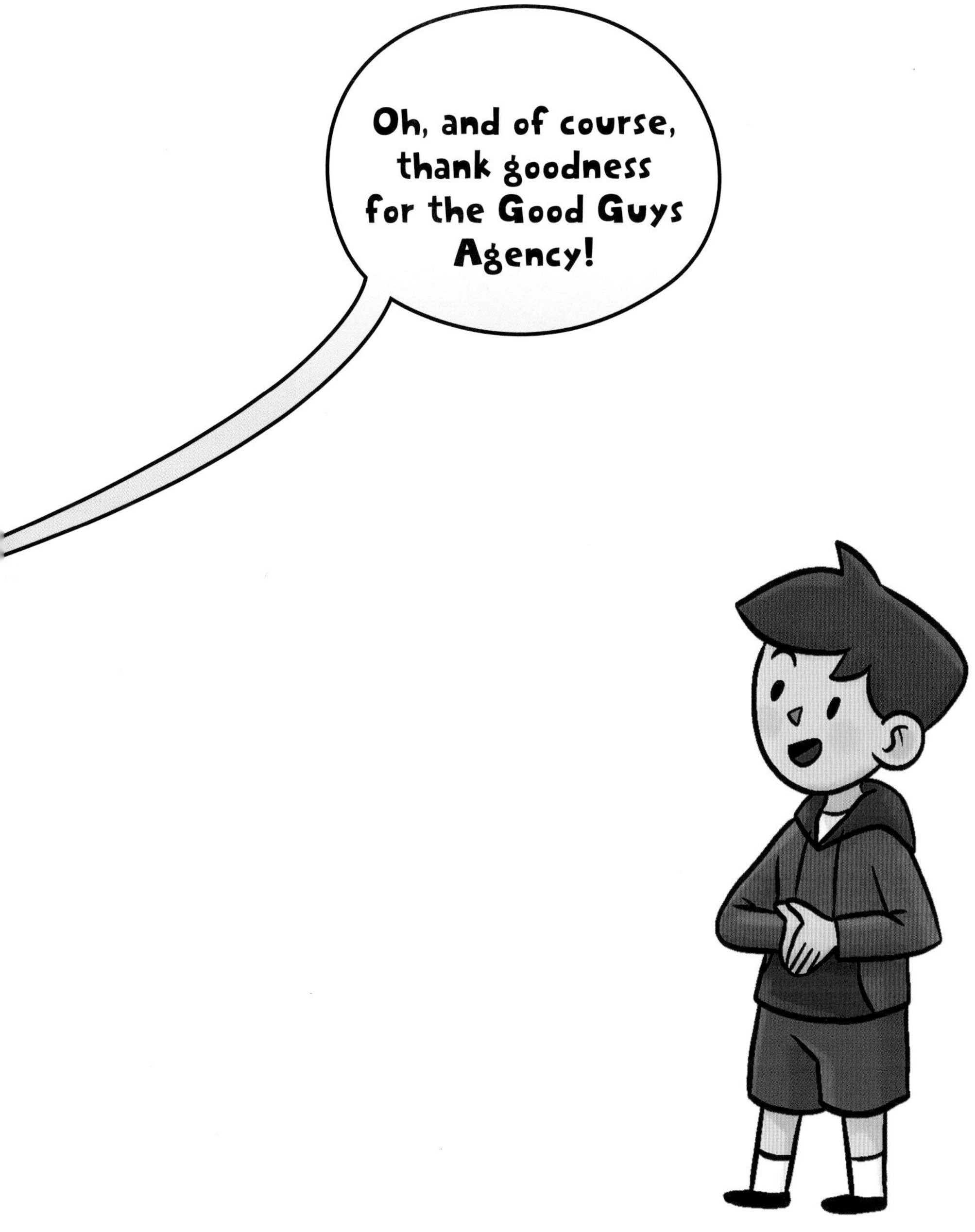
Oh, and of course, thank goodness for the Good Guys Agency!

"That's right! Another case is in the books!" Lucky said. "Speaking of books . . . Red! We have to help Rudy get the case into the book. We have to go!"

"Bye, Charlie. Bye, Teddy," Red shouted as Lucky dragged him back to the Kid Cruiser.

Charlie and Teddy began to build Fort Crumble for the sixth—and last—time.

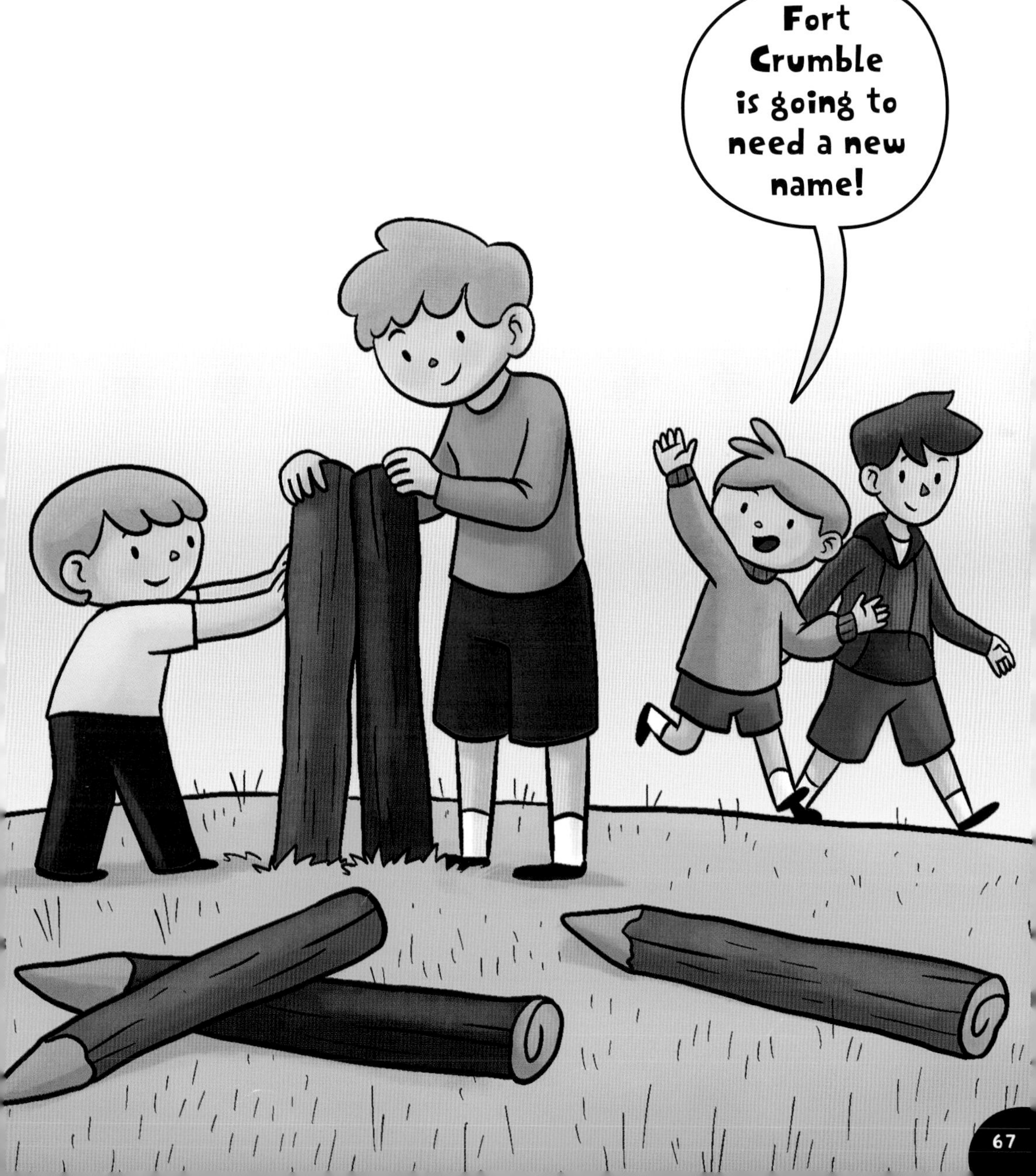
Fort Crumble is going to need a new name!

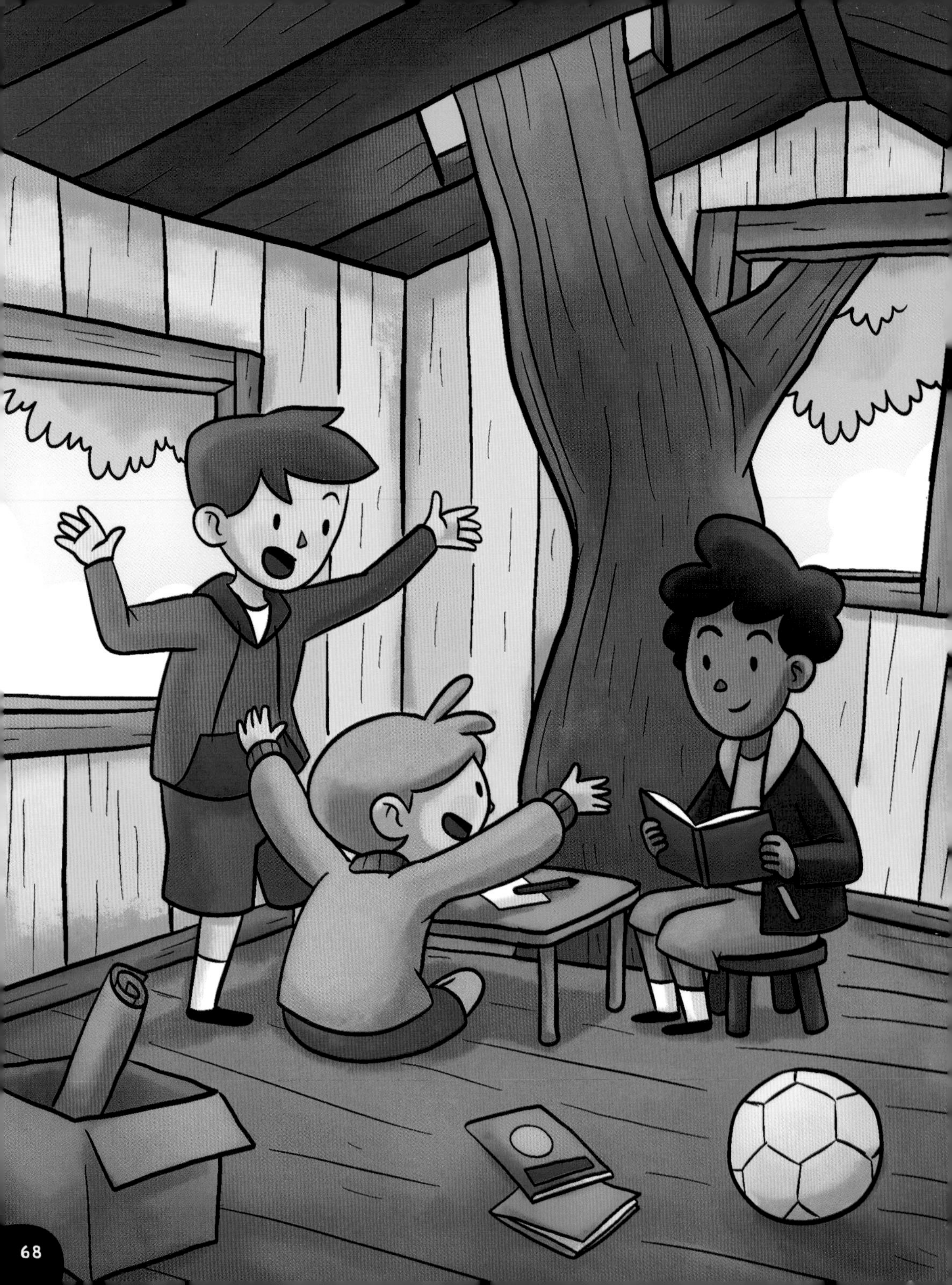

CHAPTER EIGHT

The One Thing

"We got to see where Mr. Rogers grew up and . . ." Red was saying, as Rudy wrote furiously to keep up.

"Red, don't forget about the time we jumped over the stone wall!" Lucky interrupted.

"Yes, I was just getting to that. We had to help him run away from some bullies, and . . ."

By the time the sun was setting, Rudy's pencil was down to the stubbiest of stubs. But the trouble at Fort Crumble, the kindness of Fred Rogers, and the adventures of the Good Guys Agency were at last safely recorded in the Book of the Future.

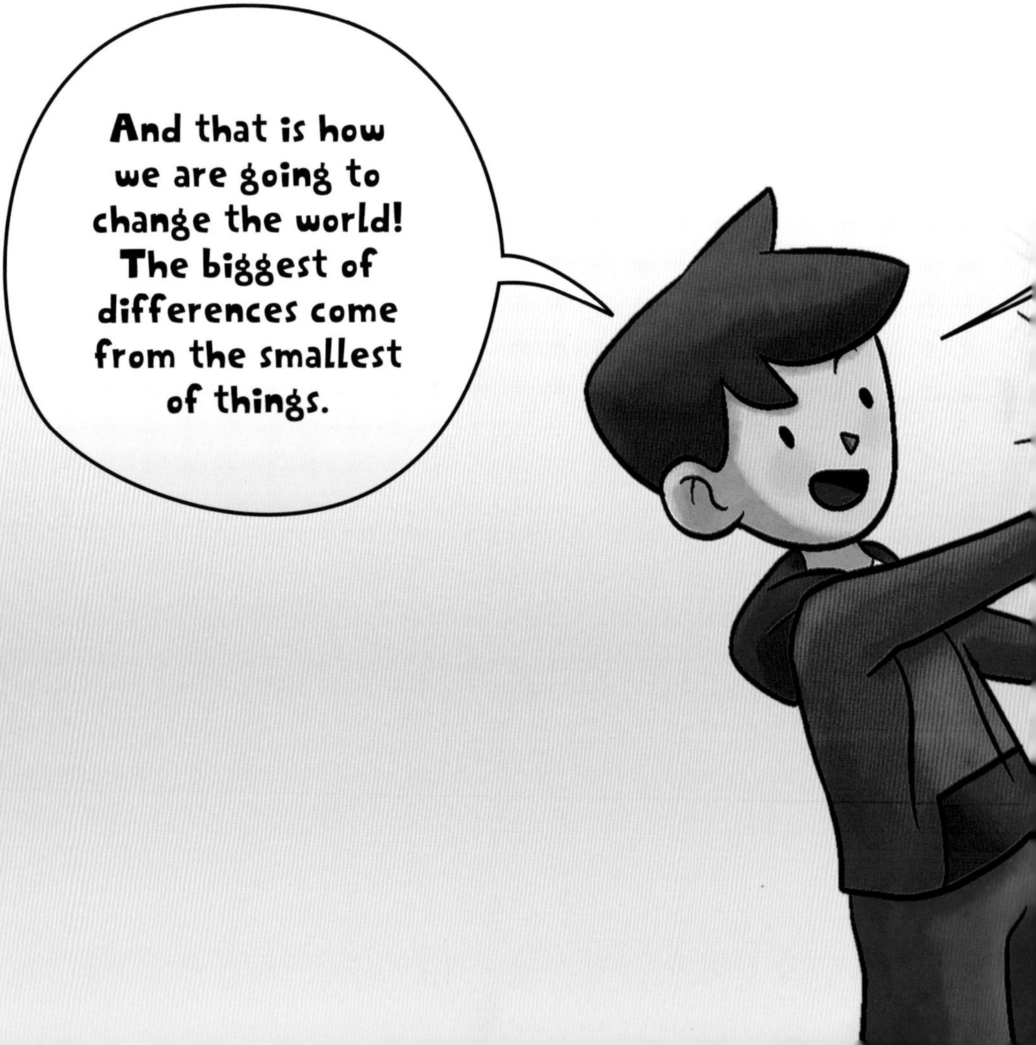
And that is how we are going to change the world! The biggest of differences come from the smallest of things.

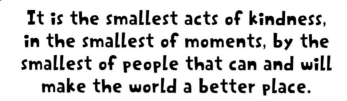

It is the smallest acts of kindness, in the smallest of moments, by the smallest of people that can and will make the world a better place.

"That's good," Red applauded. "But you're forgetting one thing."

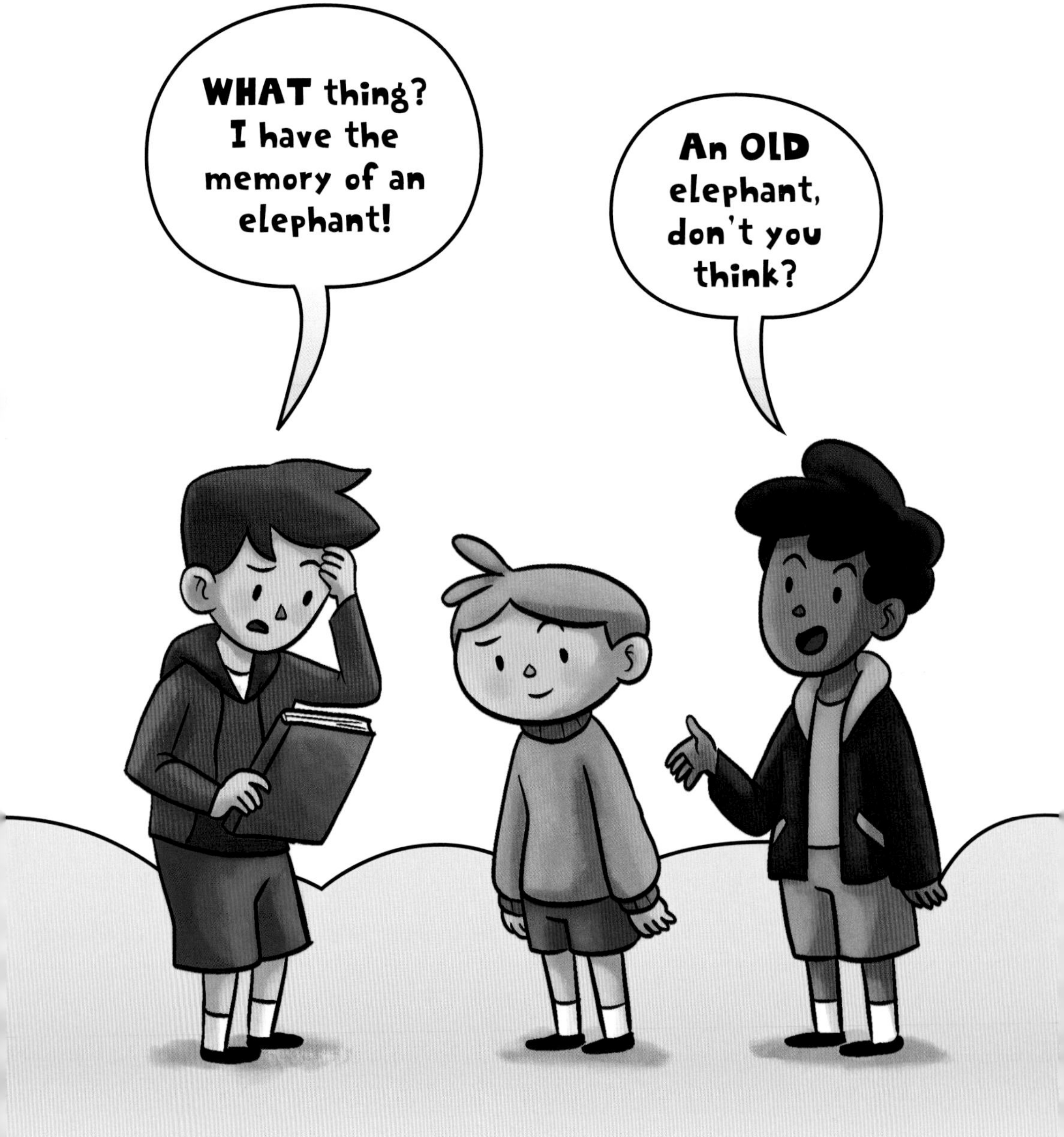
WHAT thing? I have the memory of an elephant!
An OLD elephant, don't you think?

"You forgot to tell me *THE* thing!" Red said.

"The big secret!" Rudy said.

"The thing we can't do without!" Red said.

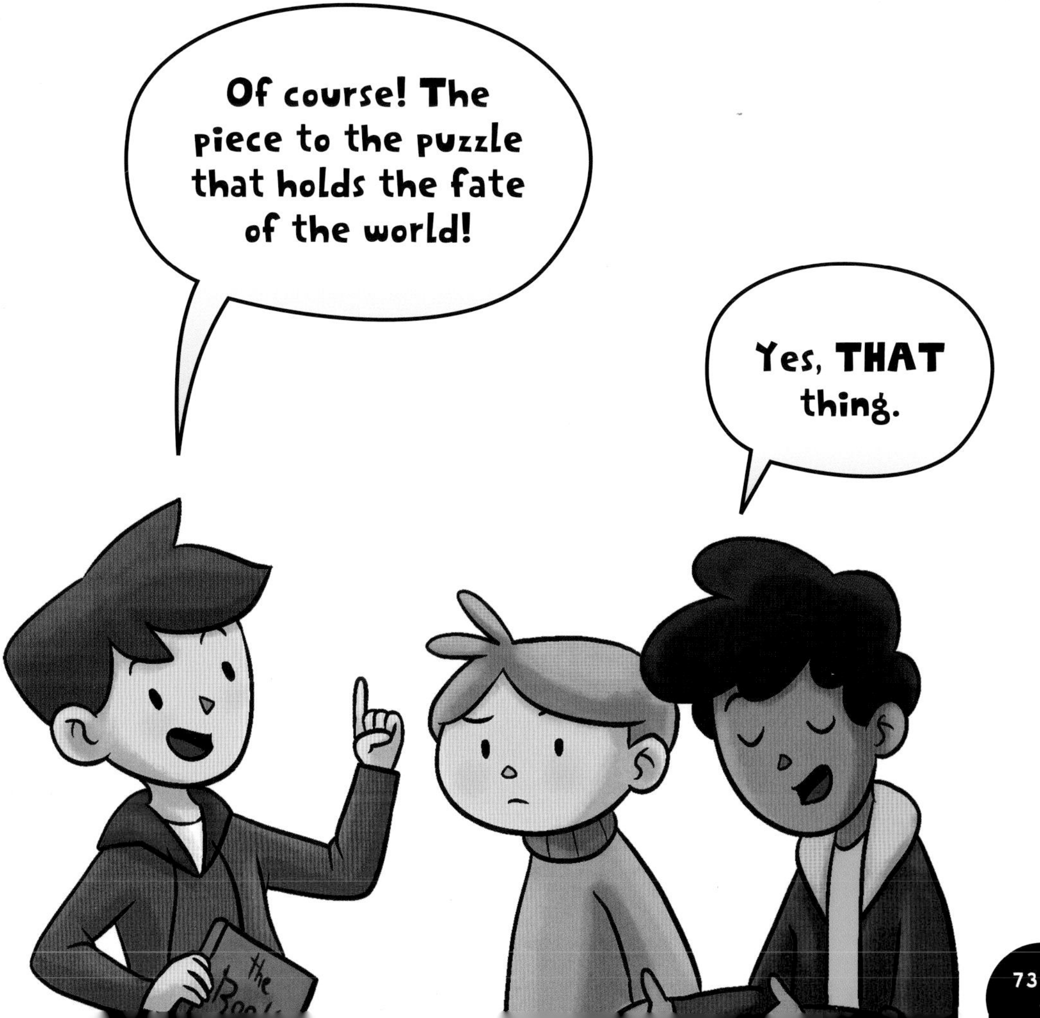
Of course! The piece to the puzzle that holds the fate of the world!
Yes, THAT thing.

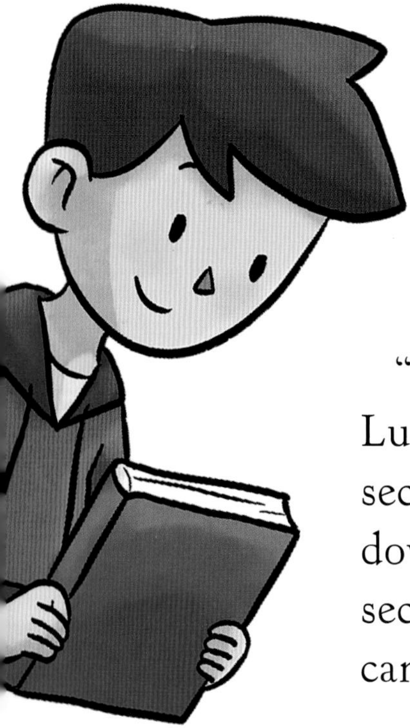

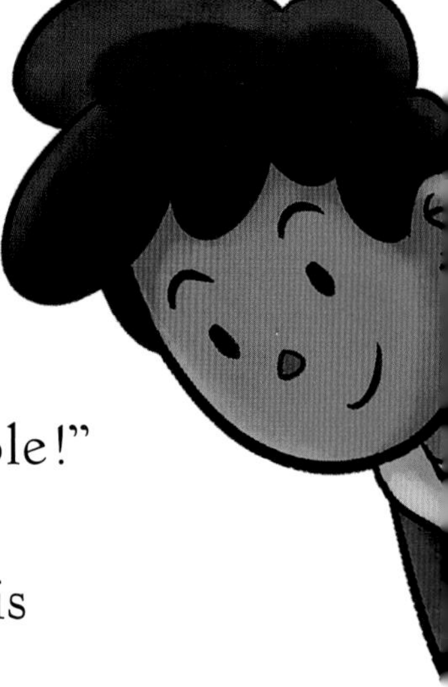

"Why, it's quite simple!" Lucky said. "Our big secret—you getting this down, Rudy? Our big secret, the one thing we can't do without, is . . . you."

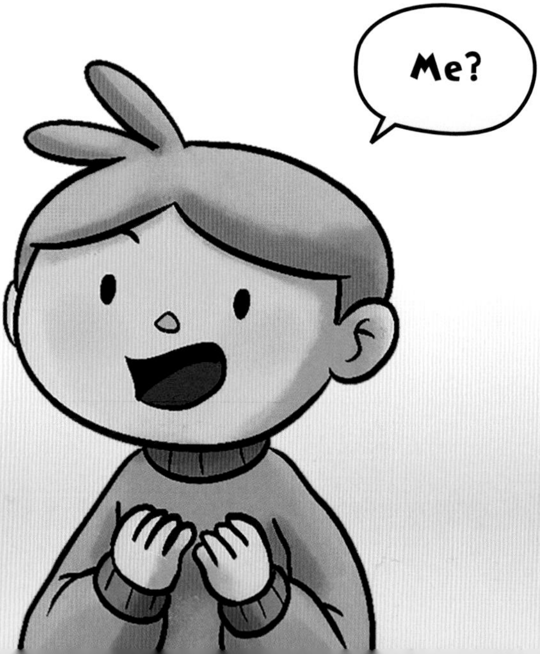
Me?

"You!" Lucky continued. "And everyone else who believes in making the world a better place. We need you to be kind to yourself and the people around you."

"We need you to do the little things every day that can make someone else's day," Rudy added. "If you can do that, then our future will be pretty sweet! The End!"

He slammed the book closed with a triumphant smile.

SLAM

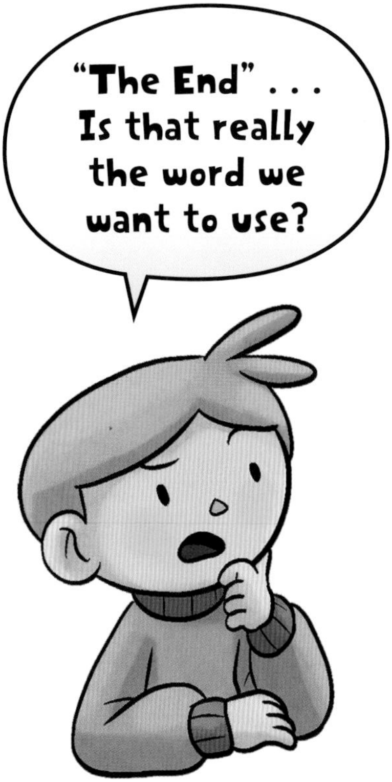
"The End" . . . Is that really the word we want to use?

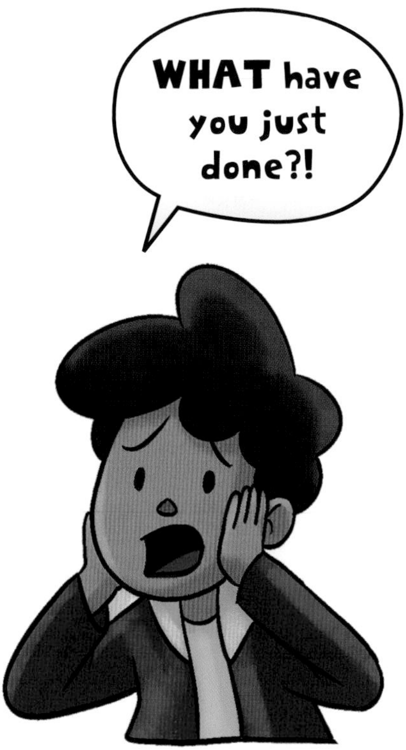
WHAT have you just done?!

But it was too late.

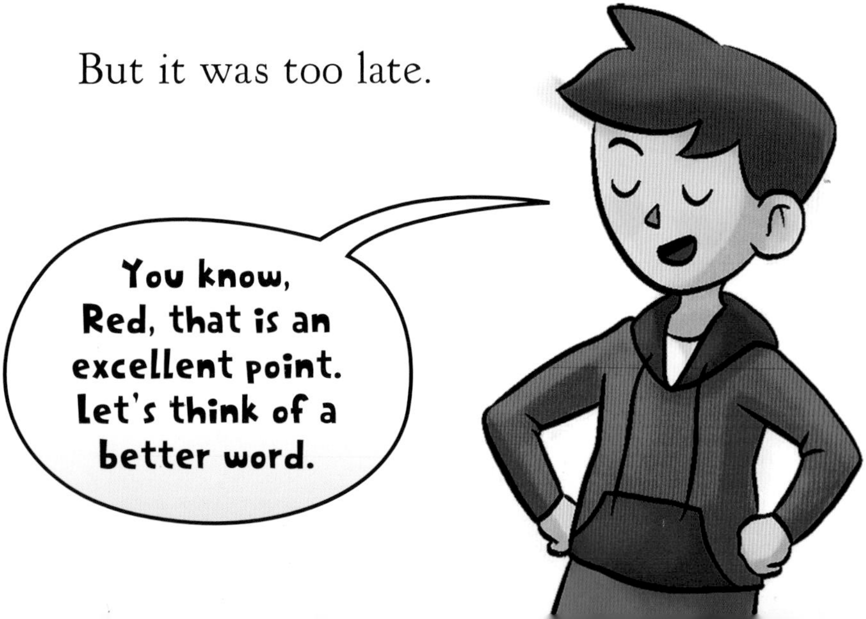
You know, Red, that is an excellent point. Let's think of a better word.

Nooooooooo
oooooooooo
ooooooooood!

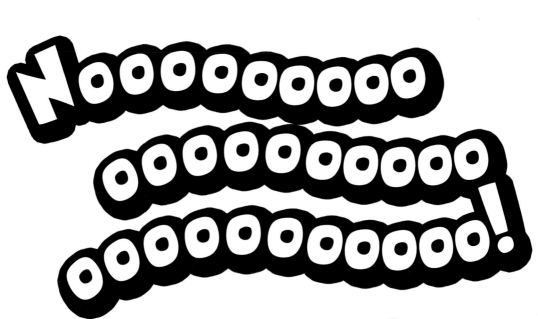

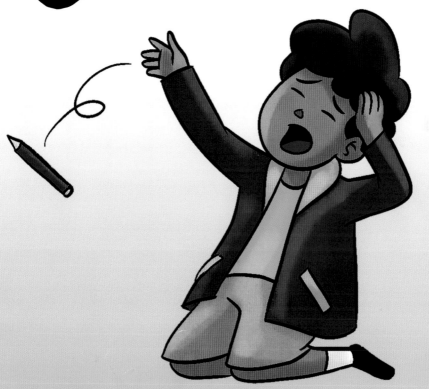

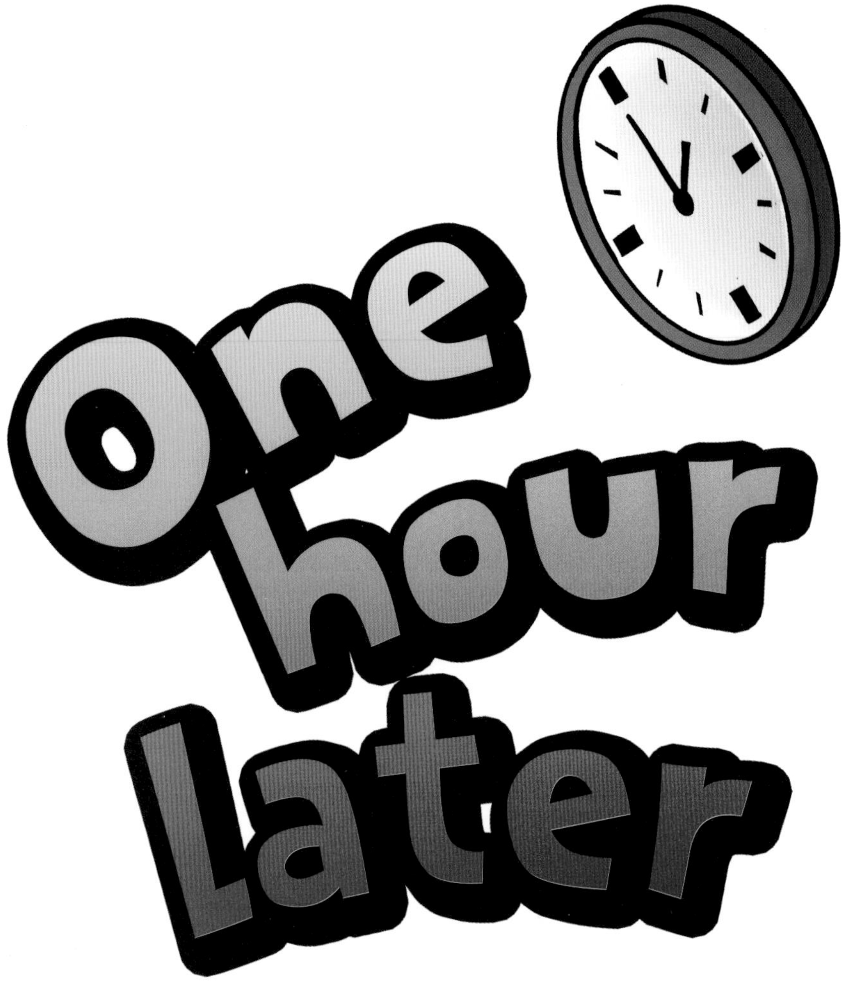

One hour later

"The End. I think 'The End' should be fine," Lucky said with confidence.

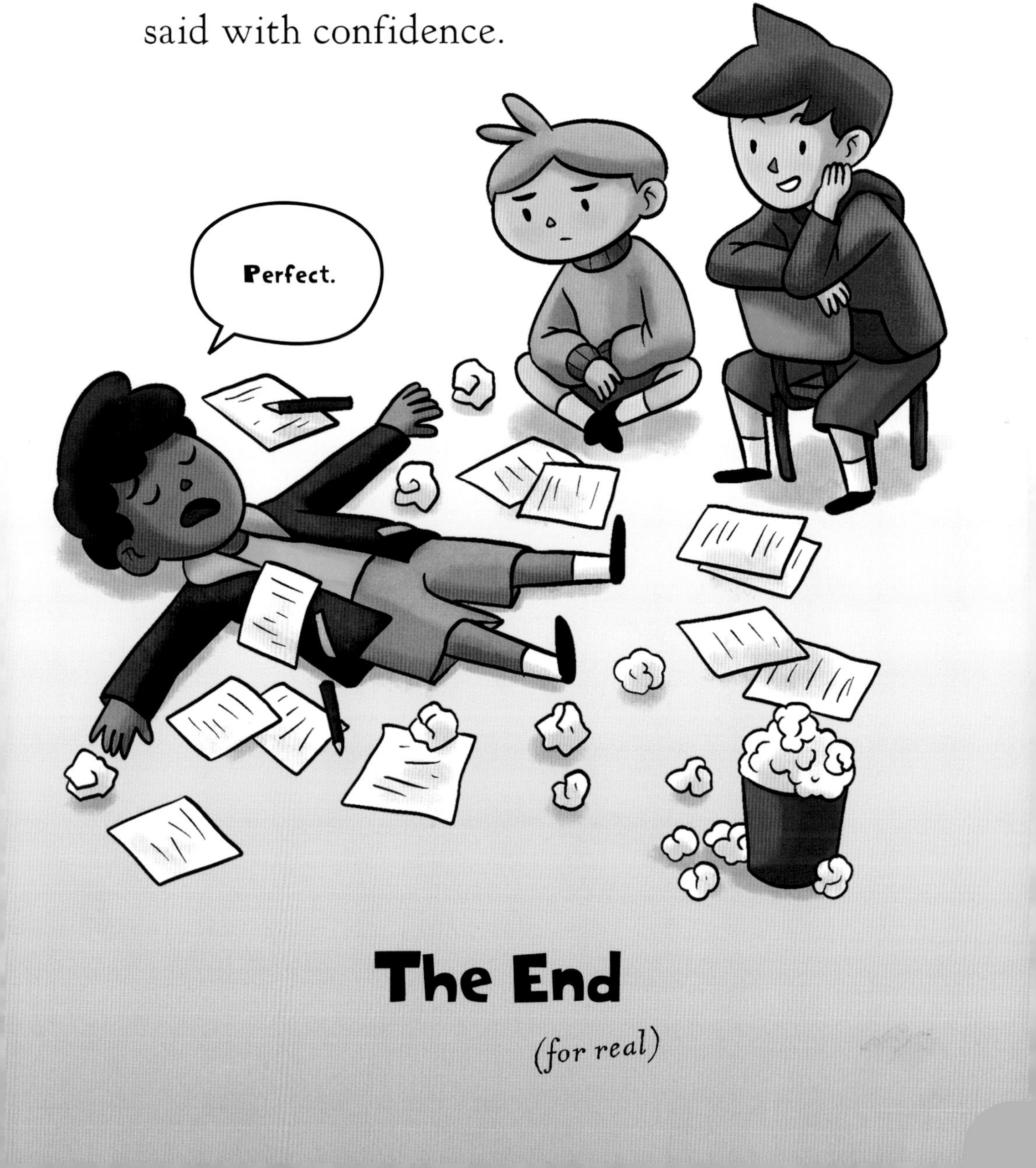
Perfect.

The End

(for real)

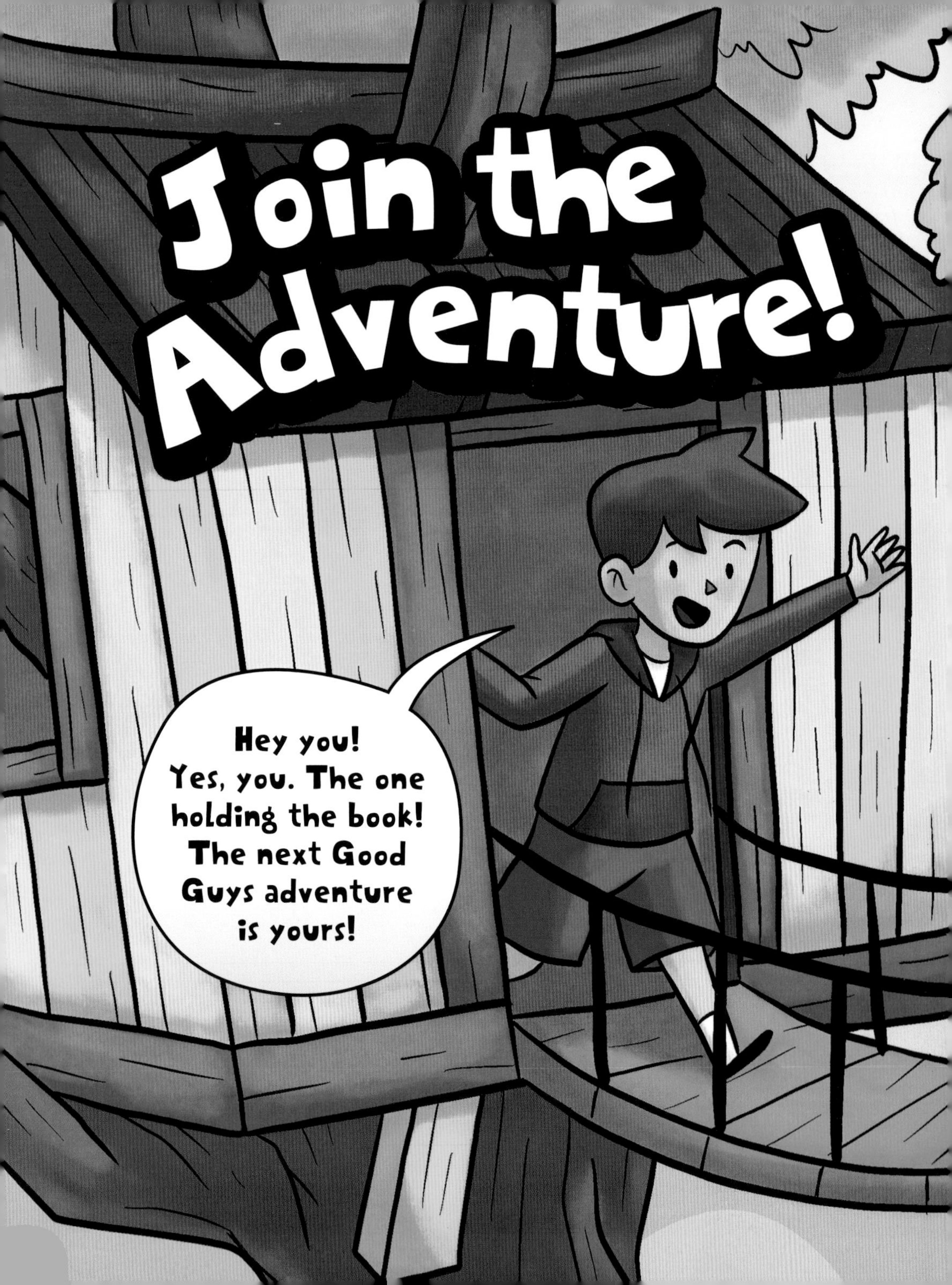
Join the Adventure!
Hey you! Yes, you. The one holding the book! The next Good Guys adventure is yours!

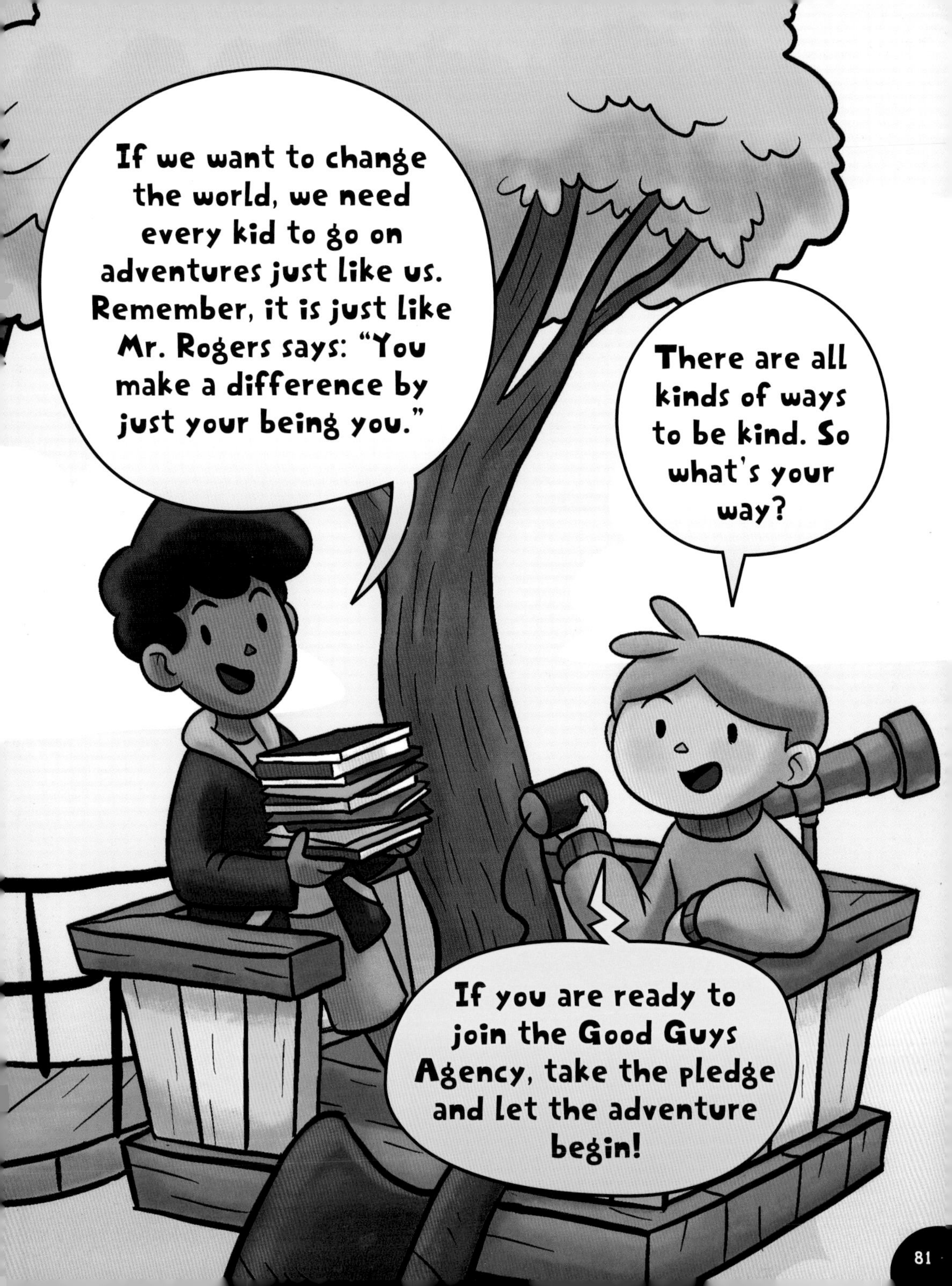
If we want to change the world, we need every kid to go on adventures just like us. Remember, it is just like Mr. Rogers says: "You make a difference by just your being you."
There are all kinds of ways to be kind. So what's your way?
If you are ready to join the Good Guys Agency, take the pledge and let the adventure begin!

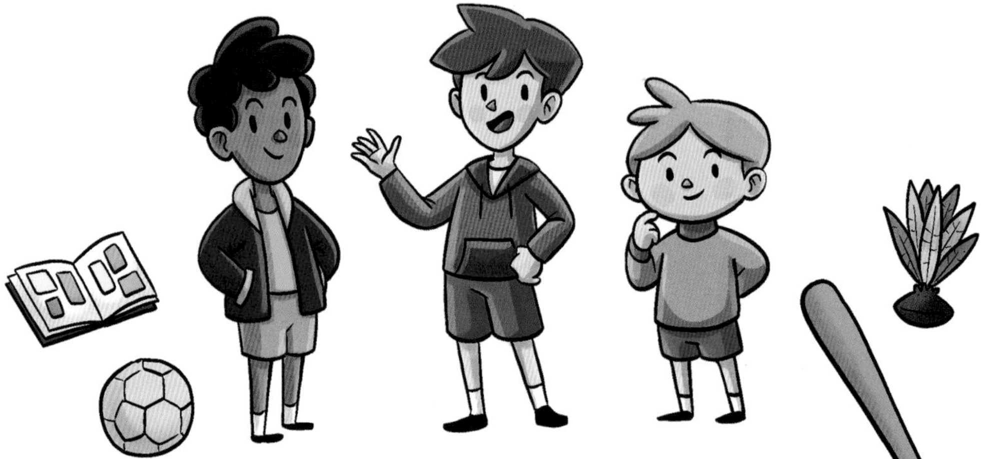

We Pledge to:

Be Kind to Others
Speak Nicely
Creatively Solve Problems
Treat Everyone with Respect
Include Others
Work Together
Love Others for Who They Are
Try New Things
Think before Reacting
Tell the Truth
Ask Questions

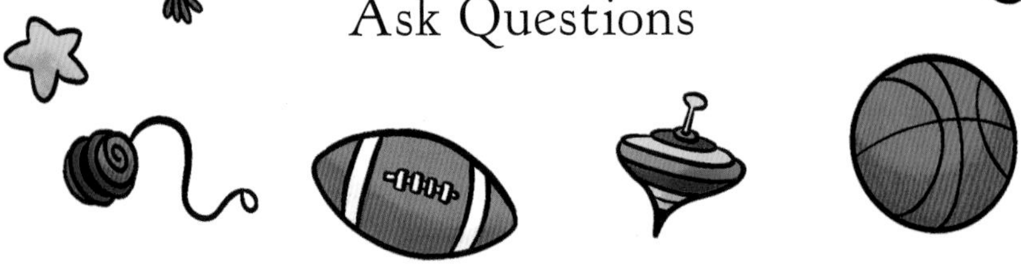

Be Positive
Always Be Learning
Take Care of Others
Apply Ourselves
Be Patient
Smile Big
Dance Goofy
Imagine for Fun

The future is now;
there is no need to wait.
Use it to help others and
good will become great.

All About Fred Rogers

F red Rogers was born in Latrobe, Pennsylvania, in 1928. Fred was an imaginative young boy who loved playing and making up stories. In 1951, he graduated from Rollins College in Winter Park, Florida, with a degree in musical composition. He moved to New York, where he worked for NBC. Fred then moved back home to work as a composer, producer, and puppeteer for a local television station.

In 1962, Fred Rogers graduated with a degree in divinity from the Pittsburgh Theological Seminary. Fred wanted to be a minister. He quickly discovered that he could do a lot of good in the world by blending his passions for television and early childhood development.

Fred Rogers and Officer François Clemmons share a foot bath.

He made his television debut in 1963 with the Canadian Broadcasting Company. Eventually, he moved the show to Pittsburgh's public television network under the name *Mister Rogers' Neighborhood*. For 905 episodes, Mister Rogers educated child audiences all over the nation. During the run of the show, Fred wore a lot of cardigans and taught children many life lessons that they'd never forget.

Fred Rogers begins his children's show.

About the Author

Nick Esposito is an award-winning teacher and education consultant with a passion for bringing best practices of service learning into the classroom. Nick has traveled around the world serving with different organizations for different cultures and peoples, from which he has developed the belief that educational experiences must sharpen the mind and embrace the heart. Nick has degrees from Villanova University (Journalism, Sociology, Peace & Justice), Johns Hopkins (Master's in Urban Education), and the University of Pennsylvania (Master's in Education Entrepreneurship). Nick is the ecstatic husband of the love of his life and "Habitat Crush," Cynthia. He is also a longtime hockey player and Philadelphia sports fan. He is the proud teacher of hundreds of students, all of whom are impacting the world in their own exciting, unique, yet quirky ways.

About the Illustrator

Ricardo Tokumoto was born in Limeira, Brazil. He moved to Belo Horizonte and attended the Faculty of Fine Arts at UFMG and graduated with a BA in Animation Cinema. Today, he works on webcomics, creates comics for authors and publishers, and also works as an illustrator and animator.

About Bushel & Peck Books

Bushel & Peck Books is a children's publishing house with a special mission. Through our Book-for-Book Promise™, we donate one book to kids in need for every book we sell. Our beautiful books are given to kids through schools, libraries, local neighborhoods, shelters, nonprofits, and also to many selfless organizations that are working hard to make a difference. So thank you for purchasing this book! Because of you, another book will make its way into the hands of a child who needs it most.

Do you know a school, library, or organization that could use some free books for their kids? We'd love to help! Please fill out the nomination form on our website (see below), and we'll do everything we can to make something happen.

www.bushelandpeckbooks.com/pages/
nominate-a-school-or-organization

If you liked this book, please leave a review
online at your favorite retailer. Honest reviews
spread the word about Bushel & Peck—and
help us make better books, too!

The Adventure Continues!

Join Lucky, Rudy, and Red in more exciting cases with the Good Guys Agency!

Boys for a The Better World
GOOD GUYS AGENCY
Kind Like Fred Rogers
BOOK-FOR-BOOK
Nick Esposito • Ricardo Tokumoto

Boys for a The Better World
GOOD GUYS AGENCY
Brave Like Jackie Robinson
BOOK-FOR-BOOK
Nick Esposito • Ricardo Tokumoto

Boys for a The Better World
GOOD GUYS AGENCY
Sweet Like Milton Hershey
BOOK-FOR-BOOK
Nick Esposito • Ricardo Tokumoto

Better Boys for The a Better World
GOOD GUYS AGENCY
Play On Like Beethoven
BOOK-FOR-BOOK
Nick Esposito • Ricardo Tokumoto

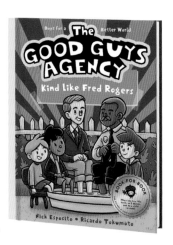

Coming Soon wherever books are sold!